Taft-Hartley Act

LANDMARK LEGISLATION

Taft-Hartley

Act

Susan Dudley Gold

Marshall Cavendish
Benchmark
New York

Other Marshall Cavendish Offices:
Marshall Cavendish International (Asia) Private Limited, 1 New Industrial Road, Singapore 536196 • Marshall Cavendish International (Thailand) Co Ltd. 253 Asoke, 12th Flr, Sukhumvit 21 Road, Klongtoey Nua, Wattana, Bangkok 10110, Thailand • Marshall Cavendish (Malaysia) Sdn Bhd, Times Subang, Lot 46, Subang Hi-Tech Industrial Park, Batu Tiga, 40000 Shah Alam, Selangor Darul Ehsan, Malaysia

Marshall Cavendish is a trademark of Times Publishing Limited

All websites were available and accurate when this book was sent to press.

Library of Congress Cataloging-in-Publication Data
Gold, Susan Dudley.
The Taft-Hartley Act / By Susan Dudley Gold.
p. cm. — (Landmark legislation)
Includes bibliographical references and index.
ISBN 978-1-60870-488-0 (Print) ISBN 978-1-60870-710-2 (eBook)
1. United States. Labor Management Relations Act, 1947—Juvenile literature. 2. Labor laws and legislation—United States—Juvenile literature. I. Title.
KF3369.85.G65 2012
344.7301–dc22

2010023505

Publisher: Michelle Bisson
Art Director: Anahid Hamparian
Series Designer: Sonia Chaghatzbanian
Photo research by Custom Communications, Inc.

Cover: Janitors face police officers clad in riot gear during a strike in Los Angeles in 2000. p. 2: Union members hold up "I want to work" placards during a labor rally in Los Angeles in 2010. p. 3: Union members throng Union Square, New York City, during May Day demonstration in 1913.

Cover photo: Getty Images/Joe Raedle
The photographs in this book are used by permission and through the courtesy of: Getty Images/Joe Raedle: cover; Mark Ralston/AFP/Getty Images, 2; Library of Congress: 3, 6, 12, 21, 23, 29 (top and bottom), 33, 46, 56, 62; North Wind Picture Archives: 27; Granger: 38 (inset), 38; Associated Press: 49, 73, 77, 78, 88, 93, 106, 112; AP/Damian Carl Linde, 64; AP/Dovarganes, 120; NARA, American Cities Collection: 58.

Printed in Malaysia (T)
1 3 5 6 4 2

Contents

Members attend the sixth biennial convention of the National Women's Trade Union League in 1917. The women's union, which attracted working-class members as well as wealthy donors, lent support to women strikers and participated in the suffrage movement to win voting rights for women.

Leveling the Playing Field or a Slave Labor Law?

On June 23, 1947, the U.S. Congress overrode President Harry S. Truman's veto and overwhelmingly passed the National Labor Relations Act. Known as the Taft-Hartley Act, the legislation has set the tone for labor relations ever since.

Employers celebrated the law's passage as a way to regain some control over workers and powerful unions. The act, they said, would level the playing field between employer and employee. Labor leaders referred to the act as the "slave labor law" and predicted it would destroy unions.

Congress enacted the bill after national strikes crippled the nation's economy and amid growing public anger at labor unions for disruptions in trade. The law amended the Wagner Act, the 1935 law that established the right of workers to form unions and to negotiate as a group when dealing with employers, a system called collective bargaining. The Taft-Hartley Act reaffirmed the Wagner Act's policy that collective bargaining was the best way to settle labor issues and that it was in the national interest to support that system. But it also put new restrictions on unions and took away some of their most effective bargaining tools. The act allowed the president to seek court orders to halt strikes and require lengthy cooling-off periods while government mediators worked out settlements. The Taft-Hartley Act also banned some strikes and other union actions, set up a complex system of rules governing union organizing and operations, and gave states the right to pass laws limiting union membership.

Still in force today, the Taft-Hartley Act has turned out to be neither the employers' equal rights law, nor the unions' slave labor law. On the whole, the act gave more control to employers and the government, tipping the balance of power away from unions. The law made it more difficult for unions to organize workers, thus reducing their effectiveness at the bargaining table. Strikes became less common as union membership decreased and court rulings gave employers the right to hire permanent replacements for workers on strike.

The act did not return workers to the slavelike conditions of a previous era or destroy the labor movement. Its passage did mark the beginning of a dramatic decrease in union membership, however. Critics contend that unions have outlived their usefulness and will eventually die out altogether.

Whether that happens or not, labor unions have played an important role in improving the lot of American workers. They began in America's first days as an independent nation and have endured adverse court rulings, antilabor employers, armed strikebreakers, and restrictive legislation. More than six decades after the Taft-Hartley Act passed amid predictions that the law would destroy the labor movement, unions continue to negotiate better terms for workers, play a role in national politics, and make their mark on the U.S. economy.

Glossary

antitrust legislation—A law designed to prevent or regulate monopolies.

arbitration—Method of settling disputes in which an impartial person decides the outcome. Usually both parties are required to abide by the decision.

boycott—Action in which workers and others cease doing business with a company involved in a labor dispute. Those involved in a boycott stop buying goods from a company and refuse to work for the firm or handle its products.

card check—System in which workers sign cards to show they want a union to represent them at the workplace. The cards are checked off on a list of employees, and if a majority favors the union, the National Labor Relations Board (NLRB) conducts an election. Employers may choose to recognize the union without holding a formal election.

closed shop—A workplace where the employer has agreed, as part of a union contract, to hire only employees who belong to the union. Outlawed under Taft-Hartley.

collective bargaining—Method by which workers negotiate terms of their employment as a group rather than individually.

company union—An organization of employees formed by the company and whose actions are controlled or influenced by management; outlawed under Taft-Hartley.

contract—Legal document detailing terms of employment (wages, benefits, working conditions, and so forth).

craft union—Group representing workers who possess the same skill, such as plumbers or welders.

featherbedding—Union requirement to hire more workers than necessary for a job, or to adopt work procedures that appear to be pointless, complex, and time-consuming, merely to employ additional workers.

industrial union—Workers' group representing employees in one industry, such as steelworkers, regardless of workers' particular skills.

injunction—Court order; filed in labor cases to stop a strike or other action and require employees to return to work.

jurisdictional strike—A strike called when two or more unions are involved in a dispute over which one is the legitimate representative of workers at a workplace.

lockout—When an employer closes down the business and "locks out" employees from the workplace as a result of a labor dispute. Also called a shutout.

mediation—Method of settling disputes in which an impartial third party works with union and management to reach a voluntary agreement. Also called conciliation.

monopoly—When a company or group has exclusive control over a market or service.

open shop—A workplace that allows workers to choose whether or not to belong to a union; nonmembers do not have to pay union dues, but unions are required to represent members and nonmembers equally.

picketing—A person or group of people standing outside a plant or other business protesting about an issue or trying to persuade others not to enter during a strike.

racketeering—Engaging in dishonest or other criminal activities.

replacement workers—Employees hired by a company to replace striking workers during a labor dispute.

right-to-work laws—State laws that ban labor contracts that require workers to join unions or pay union fees as a condition of employment.

secondary boycott/strike/picketing—Boycott, strike, or picketing by a union against a business with which it has no dispute in an effort to pressure that firm to stop doing business with the employer involved in the labor dispute; for example, a boycott against a department store that sells suits made by a company that is involved in a labor dispute with a garment workers' union. Outlawed by Taft-Hartley.

sit-down strike—An illegal demonstration in which workers refuse to leave a workplace during a labor dispute.

strike—Temporary work stoppage to protest an unfair labor practice or to resolve a labor dispute.

supervisor—An employee responsible for management tasks, such as hiring, firing, recommending such actions, and directing the work of other employees. Unions cannot represent supervisors under the terms of Taft-Hartley.

sweatshop—A factory or workshop, especially in the clothing industry, in which employees work long hours under poor conditions for little pay.

unfair labor practices—Employer or union activities labeled as unfair in state and federal labor relations legislation. For employees, these include closed shops and secondary strikes, boycotts, and picketing; for employers, they include threats or discriminating against union organizers or employees, blocking union organizing, and running company unions.

union security clause—Section of a collective bargaining agreement that protects the union; for example, a clause requiring all employees (members and nonmembers) to pay for collective bargaining.

union shop—Workplace where all workers are required to join the union once they pass the trial period and become full-fledged employees.

wildcat strike—A work stoppage not sanctioned by the union.

yellow-dog contract—An agreement that forces a worker to pledge not to join a union in order to get a job.

Laborers waiting for jobs gather at a labor exchange in New York in 1868.

CHAPTER ONE

Early Union Efforts

Immigrants who first sought refuge in North America in the 1600s and 1700s saw the new territory as a land of freedom and free enterprise. The poor immigrants who flocked to the new land seeking opportunity, however, soon found that workers had little freedom to pursue their dreams. Some exchanged a voyage to America for work to be performed once they arrived in the new land. Others signed on with tradesmen as indentured servants after they came to America, pledging to work for a set number of years under slavelike conditions in exchange for learning a trade. Still others contracted to work as field hands or at other pursuits that required long hours for little pay.

When these voluntary workers did not fill the needs of colonial America, the wealthy landowners and merchants sought help from other sources. Unscrupulous brokers in England and the rest of Europe tricked poor people into signing contracts as indentured servants and shipped them to America. Some brokers kidnapped children and sent them overseas or persuaded young paupers to board the ships heading for the colonies. In addition, European officials sent paupers and prisoners to the New World as workers.

The journey across the ocean for both voluntary and involuntary immigrants was a nightmarish experience. Disease, seasickness, and hunger afflicted the travelers. Crowded aboard small, unsanitary vessels, many of the would-be workers died during the passage. Those who survived encountered harsh conditions upon arrival. Once in America, people who had arranged to work as indentured servants joined their masters to begin their employment. Those who owed money for their passage were sold to the highest bidder. Typically adults had to work for four to seven years to pay off their debts. Children were bound to masters from one to seven years. As grim as their lives were, however, they were better off than the people captured in Africa, who were enslaved for life.

Good masters taught their servants a trade and treated them fairly. Unfortunately, too many masters found it easy to take advantage of their indentured workers. Some masters whipped servants, did not feed and clothe them adequately, and worked them to exhaustion. A number of workers died at the hands of unscrupulous masters.

When the conditions became unbearable, dissatisfied workers sometimes banded together to protest. Small groups of workers went on strike or refused to report for work; indentured servants sometimes schemed to run away from their masters. Most of these actions flared up quickly in response to a specific incident and faded away within a few days.

A few abused workers took their masters to court. Unlike African slaves, white indentured servants had the right to sue. Colonial courts usually sided with employers, however, and dealt harshly with protesting workers. Under the laws of the time, employers could force indentured servants and contracted employees to work. The courts ordered workers to fulfill the terms of their contracts no matter how onerous the conditions. In some colonies employees who refused to work or took other actions to protest an employer's unfair treatment could be prosecuted in criminal court. Such court actions prevented workers from forming permanent coalitions to address general conditions.

EARLY LABOR LAWS AND COURT RULINGS

The first labor laws in America focused not on protecting workers from unfair conditions but on protecting employers and customers from high wages. During the 1600s workers were in such high demand in the North American colonies, especially in New England, that wages soared. After indentured servants had worked the years required by contract, they won their freedom.

In many cases, masters gave their former workers money or livestock and sometimes land for their service. Some opened their own businesses or continued working in their trade for a regular salary. The lure of cheap land and adventure tempted many to abandon their trade and move west. The tradesmen who remained in the East could charge high fees for their work. In 1630 Massachusetts officials responded by setting a limit on wages for tradesmen and day laborers. The law also required workers to labor "the whole day."

A law passed forty years later retained the same rate of pay for tradesmen for a ten-hour day, not including time off for lunch. The Puritan authorities believed that long hours and low wages protected workers from the sins of drunkenness and idleness and prevented them from buying clothing and other goods "above their station."

During the 1700s craftsmen and day laborers served a vital role in providing a variety of services to the growing colonies. Bakeries, hat shops, printing companies, breweries, gunpowder manufacturers, grain mills, and linen factories all employed workers. Itinerant blacksmiths, peddlers, and farm laborers performed needed jobs throughout the colonies. With increasing demand for workers of all sorts, wages again began to rise. As before, New England officials attempted to squelch the increase in pay. In 1776, as Americans declared their independence and went to war against Great Britain, officials from Massachusetts, New Hampshire, Rhode Island, and Connecticut forged a compact to control wages and prices in the four New England states.

Initially the agreement won the approval of the Continental Congress, formed to unite the states in their war effort. After the war, however, Congress changed its view and urged the repeal of such laws. The new American leaders condemned the laws as a "grievous Oppression of Individuals." Nevertheless, independence did not improve conditions for workers. Wages decreased in the economic downturn that followed the Revolutionary War, and even skilled craftsmen found their livelihoods threatened. To protect their interests, skilled workers began to form unions to increase their power when dealing with employers. By the end of the 1700s, unions had taken several actions to win wage increases and improvements in work conditions for their members.

In response, the new Congress, whose members included several influential businessmen, passed the Combination Acts of 1799 and 1800. The legislation prohibited the formation of a workplace group, such as a labor union, that would act on behalf of its members. Those who violated the law were subject to arrest as criminals. The acts also covered employers, but officials and the court applied the ban only to labor unions. In addition, the courts accepted the doctrine, based on British common law, that the formation of such workplace groups for the purpose of overriding conditions outlined in a contract could be considered a conspiracy. Judges sympathetic to industry doled out harsh sentences to labor leaders found guilty of organizing unions and directing employee protests. For more than a century these legal tools stymied the efforts of unions to improve the lot of workers.

Shoemakers and tailors were among the first to challenge the antiunion laws. In 1785 they went on strike in New York City for three weeks to protest poor working conditions and low wages. The New York shoemakers set up the first known fund for strikers in 1805. In a case filed against Philadelphia shoemakers in 1806, a state court found the workers guilty of criminal conspiracy when they formed a union to seek higher pay. It was the first union to be tried for conspiracy. Court fines forced the union into bankruptcy and it disbanded shortly afterward. Women went on strike for the first time in 1824 after the Pawtucket, Rhode Island, factory where they worked as weavers reduced their pay and extended their workday. Three years later in 1827 a group of Philadelphia tailors, on trial for conspiracy, were found guilty of "injury to trade" for their union activities.

Workers' efforts to increase their wages began to draw support from the public in the 1830s and 1840s. Many Americans spoke out against the practice of convicting workers merely because they formed unions to negotiate for raises in pay. An 1842 decision in *Commonwealth* v. *Hunt* by the Massachusetts Supreme Court reflected a more tolerant view of unions by the court. The ruling, a landmark in labor law, for the first time gave unions legal standing. It also established unions' right to strike and to set up closed shops for the purpose of improving wages and other work conditions. A closed shop is one in which all employees are required to be union members in good standing. *Commonwealth v. Hunt* involved a bootmakers' union in Boston headed by John Hunt and six other men. The union threatened a strike if a factory owner did not fire a worker who had broken union rules. The dismissed worker complained to the state. The Massachusetts attorney general took the case to court, claiming that union members had participated in an illegal conspiracy. The lower court found the union guilty, but the state's high court overruled the decision. The opinion, written by Massachusetts Chief Justice Lemuel Shaw, declared that unions had a right to exist and to negotiate for better wages. The court noted that unions were not criminal conspiracies and that their attempt to seek better work conditions could not be considered an illegal act.

NATIONAL LABOR EFFORTS

After the Civil War the nation's industries flourished, particularly in the North, where factories processed everything from cotton to steel. With the growth of industry came an increase in the number of unions. By this time unions dedicated to certain trades had formed national organizations, but each operated independently of the others. In 1866 labor leaders formed the first national federation of unions, the National Labor Union (NLU), to unite the national unions. Black workers formed their own national federation, the Colored National Labor Union. The NLU lobbied Congress to require an eight-hour workday, but the campaign was largely unsuccessful. The NLU lost much of its support when it reinvented itself as labor's political party. The federation collapsed in 1873 during an economic depression that hit the nation. It served, however, to set the stage for other national labor organizations that followed.

The Knights of Labor, officially the Noble and Holy Order of the Knights of Labor, became a powerful national organization for labor after it formed in 1869. At first the Knights of Labor practiced elaborate rituals at meetings, which they kept secret to protect leaders and members from union-busting employers. Later, the group operated in the open and leaders spoke their views to win public support for the labor cause. The Knights welcomed skilled and unskilled laborers, women, and blacks. Formed by a group of Philadelphia tailors headed by Uriah S. Stephens, the Knights wanted to change the economic system to give workers more power and to prevent a handful of capitalists from controlling the nation's wealth. To accomplish that, they advocated replacing the wage system with cooperatives that spread the wealth among workers. Among other things, the organization called for the establishment of a Bureau of Labor Statistics, laws that treated labor and management equally, measures to protect workers' health and safety, recognition of labor unions as the official representatives of workers, equal pay for men and women doing the same work, and a ban on hiring children younger than fifteen to work in mines and factories. The group opposed the import of foreign workers, particularly Chinese laborers, who were excluded from membership in the Knights of Labor.

In its early years, the Knights of Labor opposed strikes, instead supporting the use of arbitration as a way to resolve labor disputes. The organization later adopted the strategy of work stoppages in successful strikes against the Union Pacific Railroad in 1884 and the Wabash Railroad in 1885. The union's victories increased its prestige among workers. By 1886 the national union, under Terence V. Powderly's leadership, boasted 700,000 members. That year, on May 1, the Knights and other labor groups took part in a massive one-day strike to support the eight-hour day. More than 350,000 workers participated nationwide, the largest strike the country had ever witnessed.

On May 3, the Monday after the national strike, police killed two striking workers during a confrontation outside a plant in Chicago. The following day, at a rally to protest the deaths, a bomb went off in the crowd gathered in the Haymarket section of Chicago. The blast and the rioting that followed killed seven police officers, injured sixty more, and led to as many civilian casualties.

Anarchists had set up the rally, and police began rounding up dozens of men and women suspected of belonging to the radical group. Anarchists believe in a voluntary system of society with no formal government. They have been active in the labor movement as well as many other causes, including antiwar efforts, the abolition of slavery, and civil rights. In a well-publicized and controversial trial, eight anarchists were convicted of murder in connection with the bombing. Four were later executed. Critics contend that the legal proceedings were seriously flawed and that the men were wrongly convicted for their beliefs.

Although no evidence linked the Knights of Labor to the bombing, many Americans blamed the labor movement and the Knights in particular for the attack. The Haymarket affair further weakened the Knights when members split over whether to support the anarchists, who had been

A protest over the deaths of two strikers erupted into violence in the Haymarket section of Chicago in 1886. The riot claimed the lives of seven police officers; dozens of strikers and officers suffered injuries in the clash.

involved in the labor movement. Powderly tried to distance his organization from the anarchists. "Honest labor is not to be found in the ranks of those who march under the red flag of anarchy, which is the emblem of blood and destruction," he declared after the incident. "It is the duty of every organization of working men in America to condemn the outrage committed in Chicago in the name of labor." Others, however, believed the labor movement should stand behind workers in the cause, regardless of their personal philosophies. Samuel Gompers, another labor leader, worked hard to win clemency for the convicted men. Three of them were eventually released; a fourth committed suicide in jail.

After the Haymarket riot, membership in the Knights began to decline, and public support eroded. A falling out among

Mother Jones:

Mary Harris Jones, better known as Mother Jones, was "the miner's angel," or "the grandmother of all agitators," depending on one's point of view. A West Virginia prosecutor once called her "the most dangerous woman in America."

Wearing a long black dress and a black hat and carrying a purse, Mother Jones faced down irate factory owners, defied government officials, and stood up to hired thugs and armed guards. Her fearless campaign made her the "mother" of union members and the working class. Stamping her foot, she cajoled, shouted at, scolded, and at times cursed mine workers in her successful campaign to build up union membership and inspire workers to take action.

Mary Harris was born in Ireland in 1830 and immigrated to the United States with her family at age eleven. She worked as a teacher and a seamstress. Her husband, George Jones, an iron molder from Tennessee whom she married in 1860, led efforts to form a branch of one of the first unions in Memphis in 1865. He died from yellow fever in 1867. The disease also claimed all four of the couple's children.

Mary Jones headed for Chicago, a major metropolis in the fast-developing Midwest. An industrial center, Chicago was a city divided between the millionaires who owned the factories and lived in lakeside mansions and the workers and unemployed who lived in poverty in the south and west. Jones worked as a seamstress for the wealthy families in the area. During this time she attended a meeting of the Noble and Holy Order of the Knights of Labor, a national workers' organization. Jones quickly joined the group. She later resigned her membership, but for the rest of her long life, she would dedicate herself to the workers' campaign.

In 1891, when she was in her sixties, Jones—who became known as "Mother" Jones—began recruiting mine workers in Virginia and West Virginia to join the newly formed United Mine Workers (UMW) of America. The union hired her in 1897 as an organizer. At strike sites, her "dishpan brigades"

Union Crusader

of miners' wives successfully kept replacement workers from entering the mines. The women banged pots and pans, wielded mops and brooms, and screamed at the would-be strikebreakers until they gave up and left.

Courts issued injunctions to keep Mother Jones from speaking to the miners, but she defied the orders. She held secret meetings in dark fields and caves, saw her friends beaten and shot, and served time in jail, including almost three months in solitary confinement when she was eighty-three years old. In 1903 Mother Jones led two hundred child workers on a four-week march from Pennsylvania to the summer home of President Theodore Roosevelt on Long Island, New York. The campaign failed to win the president's support for child labor laws, but it turned public sympathy to the plight of the children, some of whom had lost hands and suffered other injuries on the job.

Mother Jones never abandoned the campaign, even as an old woman in her nineties. Looking back on her life, she said, "My life work has been to educate the worker to a sense of the wrongs he has had to suffer, and does suffer—and to stir up the oppressed to a point of getting off their knees and demanding that which I believe to be rightfully theirs."

various factions and a reaction against the group's radical stands contributed to the federation's decline. By the end of the century, the Knights had lost most of their members to Gompers's new national organization, the American Federation of Labor (AFL).

Gompers, an English-born cigar maker, founded the Federation of Organized Trades and Labor Unions of the United States of America and Canada in 1881. The organization became the AFL five years later. The AFL did not aim to restructure the economy. Its goals focused on job security, increased wages, shorter hours, and safe working conditions. Gompers believed workers had the right to form unions to bargain collectively for them, to strike, and to take other actions to press their demands. AFL leaders set up the organization as a federation of craft unions, each consisting of workers doing a certain job, such as tailors or electricians. They believed the craftsmen's shared interests would strengthen the national union. Gompers, who served as president of the AFL for almost forty years, resisted the push by some to accept industrial unions, whose members worked in a particular industry, such as automobile manufacturing. He believed that industrial unions had too little in common to form a strong group. The AFL first admitted a union of black workers in the 1920s; many AFL affiliates did not allow black workers to join their unions until much later.

The AFL quickly attracted member unions, including those which had once belonged to the Knights of Labor. The national union followed a conservative course and did not involve itself in national politics or efforts to change the system. By 1904 the labor group had more than 1.6 million members.

CHAPTER TWO

Unions Gain Power

At the end of the nineteenth century, labor unrest spread as workers protested the inequities in a system that brought factory owners great wealth and gave them almost total control over employees, while workers labored long hours for little pay. Work stoppages and strikes, some violent, began to make headline news.

During this time, factory owners relied heavily on the courts to put an end to labor disputes. The first antiunion court order, or injunction, granted by a U.S. court in 1877 against striking railway workers, set off a flurry of similar suits to stop union activities. In 1888 the Massachusetts Supreme Judicial Court ruled in favor of an injunction that stopped union members from picketing. For the most part, despite the *Hunt* ruling, courts favored employers, ruling that strikes and other methods used by unions violated the law and ordering workers back to work.

PULLMAN'S STRIKE OF 1894

A small protest by Chicago rail workers in 1894 flared into a national strike, reinforcing federal opposition to strikes and other union activity. The strike occurred in Chicago, the center of America's rail system. By the time it ended, the work action had erupted into a riot that claimed the lives of several workers and cost the railroads more than $5 million (worth approximately $129 million in present-day purchasing power) in damages and lost revenue. One hundred thousand workers forfeited almost $1.4 million in lost wages.

The strike began when workers at the Pullman Palace Car Company, the plant that manufactured Pullman rail cars, had their pay cut by 25 percent. The workers were required to live in a company town near Chicago, where the Pullman Company owned most of the buildings, including the workers' homes. Workers asked the company to lower their rent because of the wage cut. When Pullman refused and fired three of the employees who had made the request, workers went on strike. The next day, May 11, the company closed the plant.

The workers' union belonged to a national organization, the American Railway Union (ARU), run by socialist labor leader Eugene V. Debs. When the Pullman company refused to negotiate, Debs called for other ARU union members to stop handling cars made by Pullman. Almost all of the nation's railways used cars made by the company. On June 26 switchmen refused to switch the tracks for trains hauling Pullman cars, and rail traffic around the country came to a standstill.

The U.S. attorney general ordered ARU leaders to stop "compelling or inducing by threats, intimidation, persuasion, force or violence, railway employees to refuse or fail to perform duties." This order, called the Omnibus Indictment, made

Freight cars burn during the Pullman strike in Chicago in 1894. The work action claimed the lives of several workers and cost the railroads millions of dollars in damages and lost revenue.

it a federal crime for unions to persuade workers to go on strike and for union leaders to communicate with their striking members. The federal order based its authority on the fact that the strike interfered with interstate commerce and the delivery of U.S. mail. When the strike continued, a federal court declared the workers in contempt and ordered them back to work. That, too, failed to end the strike, and President Grover Cleveland ordered federal troops to Chicago.

The arrival of federal troops on July 3 enraged the striking workers, who had been conducting a peaceful demonstration. They attacked the trains carrying the troops and the melee escalated into a riot. The mob tipped over rail cars, ignited fireworks, and built barricades across the tracks. During the chaos that followed, several large buildings burned and hundreds of rail cars and other rail property were destroyed.

Company

One old folk song details the tribulations of a mine worker who wails, "I owe my soul to the company store." For many of the laborers who worked in the coal mines of Virginia and West Virginia, life revolved around the companies that owned the mining operations. The companies built settlements in the rural areas near the mines, where workers and their families lived in isolation from other towns. Company-enforced rules controlled the community. Workers could not attend meetings and in some towns had to obtain company permission to entertain guests in their homes or even to read books.

While the men performed the dangerous work of mining ore, their children attended schools owned by the company that employed their fathers and studied lessons approved by the company's owners and taught by company-paid teachers. The town's doctor, minister, and store manager were also on the company payroll. Prices at some of the company stores were exorbitant, much higher than those set by merchants in independent stores. Since workers received at least some of their pay in vouchers, or "scrip," they had to shop at the company store, the only business to accept the vouchers. Wages did not cover the cost of living for many families, and workers often had to charge their purchases. That left them owing the company and bound to work in the mines until they could repay the money. Until the late 1930s, boys, some as young as eight, worked in the mines beside their fathers. Their sisters married young or worked at nearby textile mills.

The company also controlled conditions in the mines, the number of hours worked, and the wages paid. Men worked for twelve or fourteen hours a day, six days a week, in the

Mining Towns

Miners and members of their families shop at a company store (*right*) in West Virginia in 1938.

Coal miners' shanties (*below*) stand in a row near the Elk River in Bream, West Virginia, in 1921.

mines, sometimes in caverns three feet high or even less. Many died in cave-ins or explosions caused when methane gas in the mines ignited. They did not receive a salary; instead, they were paid based on the number of tons of coal they produced. In 1913 the average annual wage for miners in West Virginia amounted to $737.62 (a little over $12,000 a year in present-day purchasing power), or about $14 a week.

More than 14,000 officers reported to the scene. National Guardsmen fired on the rioters, killing several and wounding twenty or more. ARU leaders asked unions in the American Federation of Labor to join the strike, but they refused. After several days of violent encounters and arrests of strikers and their leaders, the rail workers gave up the fight. On August 2 the Pullman Company resumed work at its factory. Workers failed to get any concessions from the company.

Many workers who lost their jobs during the strike were left destitute, without jobs and dependent on handouts from sympathetic neighbors to keep from starving. Appeals to company president George Pullman to find jobs for the desperate workers did no good. Governor John P. Altgeld wrote three letters to Pullman asking that he reinstate the workers. The governor estimated that 1,600 families—approximately 6,000 people—were starving and had no means of support. Many eventually moved away in search of jobs elsewhere. With a 25 percent wage cut, those lucky enough to still have jobs lived from paycheck to paycheck, unable to save money or improve their lot. Their lives resembled those of the indentured servants of an earlier time in America's history.

A federal grand jury indicted forty-three union leaders, including Debs, on July 19 for violating the court order. The district attorney described the court action as "a wholesale rounding up of everybody and anybody concerned in the railroad strike within the jurisdiction of the Circuit Court for the Northern District of Illinois." The leaders were accused of conspiracy for ordering the strike and illegally interfering with interstate commerce. Debs and others appealed their convictions, and the case eventually reached the U.S. Supreme Court as *In re Debs*.

The Supreme Court gave a nod of approval to the antiunion

rulings of the lower courts when it decided against Debs in 1895. Justice David J. Brewer, in his majority opinion to uphold the men's conviction, declared that the government had the authority to issue the original injunction against the strike leaders and the court had the power to charge them with contempt when the strike continued. "The strong arm of the national government may be put forth to brush away all obstructions to the freedom of interstate commerce or the transportation of the mails," Brewer wrote. Debs and his codefendants served six months in jail on the charges.

MORE ANTIUNION COURT RULINGS

The Omnibus Indictment that prohibited workers from striking, and the Supreme Court decision that upheld it, set the tone for court rulings on labor issues until 1935, when Congress passed the Wagner Act. After the *Debs* ruling, companies increasingly sought injunctions in both state and federal courts to prevent union activity. Between 1900 and May 1, 1930, courts issued almost 1,700 injunctions against unions and their members. Ironically, many of the injunctions relied on federal antitrust laws first enacted to prevent monopolies by big business. Congress passed the Sherman Antitrust Act in 1890 to limit the power of industrial complexes that controlled steel, oil, and other resources vital to the nation. The law barred companies (and other entities) from joining together to take actions that destroyed competition and restrained trade among states or with foreign countries. Violators faced injunctions and suits for triple damages as well as prosecution in criminal court.

Businesses used the antitrust law to their advantage in their antiunion campaigns. One noted case involved hatmakers in Danbury, Connecticut, who sought an increase in wages in the early 1900s. The American Federation of Labor organized a nationwide boycott to support the demands of the union, the United Hatters Union of North America. The manufacturer, the Danbury Hatters Company, owned by D. E. Loewe, took the local union to court to stop the boycott. When the case, known as *Loewe* v. *Lawlor*, finally reached the U.S. Supreme Court, the justices ruled against the hatmakers. Justice Melville W. Fuller, writing for a unanimous Court, found the hatters' union guilty of restraining interstate commerce in violation of the Sherman Antitrust Act, even though the local union did no business with other states. The ruling, delivered in 1908, specifically included labor unions under the organizations regulated by the Sherman Act. As a result of the Court's decision, the union was ordered to pay Loewe $80,000, triple the amount of lost profits the company blamed on the strike.

The ruling made small local unions vulnerable to huge settlements, but it strengthened the resolve of Debs and other labor leaders to continue their fight for better working conditions. In 1905 Debs joined a group of social reformers to found the Industrial Workers of the World (IWW). Its goal was to unite all the workers of the world into one powerful union. The organization aimed to eliminate the wage system and allow workers to share in the profits from their labor. Nicknamed the Wobblies, the international union attracted more than 100,000 members at the height of its power in 1917. The IWW opened its doors to all laborers, appealing especially to immigrants, women, blacks, and others who had never belonged to a union before.

Despite the setbacks in court, unions made headway in their dealings with some employers, particularly with smaller factories that did not relish the expense of a court fight. Unions

Members of the Industrial Workers of the World hold a rally in New York City's Union Square in 1914.

also had some success with state and federal legislators, who passed laws to help protect workers from the more outrageous practices of unscrupulous business owners. Legislators in New York, New Jersey, Pennsylvania, and several other states passed laws allowing workers to form unions. Other citizens, however, blamed unions for the violence that sometimes erupted during strikes, even though businesses were also implicated in the attacks. Wealthy manufacturers exerted pressure on lawmakers and the courts to continue their opposition to unions. Several states adopted laws that prohibited picketing, boycotts, and other union practices.

Even when laws protected unions, courts often ruled against them in favor of business owners. In 1908 the Supreme Court struck down a provision in the Erdman Act, passed by Congress in 1898, that barred rail companies from firing workers for joining unions. Such a provision, the Court ruled in *Adair* v. *United States*, interfered with an employer's constitutional rights to own property and make contracts. Furthermore, Congress had no power to regulate trade between the states. In an earlier case, *Lochner* v. *New York*, the Court also sided with employers when it overturned a New York law that favored workers. That ruling, issued in 1905, nullified a state statute that barred bakers from working more than sixty hours a week or ten hours a day. The Court decided, by a narrow 5 to 4 vote, that the Constitution protected the right of employers and employees to make their own contracts and set their own terms of work, and the state had no right to interfere with such agreements.

WORKERS PROTEST HARSH CONDITIONS

Meanwhile, many workers continued to labor under atrocious conditions that endangered their health and, in extreme cases, their lives. Particularly at risk were children who labored in dingy factories or at home shops. Some as young as six or seven spent their days sewing on buttons, fashioning artificial flowers, or shoveling coal for up to sixteen hours a day. By 1918 all states required children to attend school. Truant officers and state inspectors had little success, however, in tracking down the underage workers.

On November 22, 1909, twenty thousand workers in New York factories went on strike to protest the harsh working conditions in the garment industry. They demanded a 20 percent hike in pay, a regular workweek of no more than fifty-two hours, and extra pay for overtime. At the Triangle Shirt Waist Factory in New York City, a group of young Jewish seamstresses, encouraged by teenage labor organizer

Pauline Newman, formed a union and joined the strike. The factory, one of the largest garment factories in the region, had long opposed worker actions.

By the end of the strike most of the smaller companies had agreed to some of the workers' demands. The Triangle Shirt Waist Factory rejected the workers' bid for shorter hours and increased wages. Its owners did agree to several safety measures, including more fire exits and the installation of fire escapes. Two years after the strike, however, the company still had not complied with the safety demands. The Triangle factory replaced workers who had joined the union with recent immigrants from Italy, Russia, Hungary, and Germany.

FIRE!

Shortly after 4:30 p.m. on March 25, 1911, fire broke out in the Triangle Shirt Waist Factory. The blaze raged through the top three floors of the ten-story building. Because the brick structure had been fireproofed, it sustained little damage. But the workers trapped inside—mostly young girls—suffered horrendous burns or suffocated from the smoke. Some of the girls ran to the windows to escape the inferno and in desperation jumped to the pavement, 100 feet below. Their broken bodies formed a gruesome pile on the sidewalk. Another thirty or so had jumped into the elevator shaft to escape the flames; their lifeless bodies clogged access to the escape route. A second elevator had been shut down, and flames quickly blocked the stairs. Outside doors were locked, and the building's only fire escape, a flimsy structure, collapsed.

One hundred and forty-six workers died before firefighters extinguished the blaze a half hour after it had started. The bodies removed from the factory were charred beyond recognition, some merely a mound of ashes. Most of the victims

Working in the

Pauline Newman began working at the Triangle Shirt Waist Company in 1901 when she was eleven years old. At first she was pleased to be hired because the company offered full-time, year-round work. The working conditions at the factory, however, soon changed her outlook.

The employees, many of them young girls in their early teens like Newman, began work at 7:30 a.m. Their shift ended at 6 p.m., but the boss often required them to work overtime until 9 p.m. Although the regular work week ran from Monday through Saturday, the young workers frequently were expected to work on Sundays as well. Newman recalled in a letter to family members that the factory owners posted a warning sign on the wall on many Saturdays: "If you don't come in on Sunday you need not come in on Monday."

The girls received no extra pay for working overtime. Instead of money, the company gave the young employees a piece of pie for supper when they worked late. As a new employee, Newman earned $1.50 a week for what often turned out to be a seven-day week. Female workers with more experience were paid a weekly salary of around $6 (male workers earned as much as $12 a week). Whenever a worker arrived a few minutes late, the owners docked her pay. She lost further pay (or was laid off for half a day) if the manager reported she spent too much time using the bathroom (which was outside the building) or paused too long in her work. At times the owners locked the exits to prevent theft and stop workers from taking too many bathroom breaks.

Newman and the other underage employees worked as "cleaners" in the "children's corner" of the factory, where they snipped off the ends of stray threads on shirtwaist blouses sewn by other workers. The "cleaned" garments were then stacked in deep cases for inspectors to examine for flaws before being shipped to stores for sale.

When state labor inspectors came to the factory, Newman wrote, she and the other underage girls hid in the garment cases, which other workers covered with blouses. In that way, the factory owners avoided state laws that prohibited children under the age of fourteen from working in factories and stores and required them to attend school.

Workers had little choice but to endure the harsh conditions. Other factories offered the same kind of treatment, and workers who protested faced immediate dismissal. Newman became involved in the effort to unionize the factory where she worked and participated in a massive workers' strike in 1909. Like others involved in the strike, Newman lost her job; she later became a union organizer in the Northeast and Midwest.

Tarpaulins cover the bodies of textile workers who jumped to their deaths from the upper floors of the Triangle Shirt Waist Factory to escape the flames that consumed the workshop in a 1911 fire. *Inset:* a view of the factory building in New York City's Washington Square.

were girls, sixteen to twenty-three years old, who worked as stitchers in the factory. The daughters of immigrant families, many barely spoke English. Their families relied on their incomes to survive.

The factory's owners, Isaac Harris and Max Blanck, escaped with their families by running along the roof to a neighboring building. They followed a route unfamiliar to the trapped workers. Officials never determined the cause of the fire.

According to a *New York Times* account of the tragedy, the Fire Department had cited the company for not maintaining enough exits. The horror of the trapped workers and the dead girls on the sidewalk caused a public uproar over conditions at the factory. Spurred by their constituents, New York lawmakers passed several laws that required factories to take many of the safety precautions the unions had demanded.

Frances Perkins, a middle-class reformer and secretary of the New York Consumer's League, stood among other bystanders as the gruesome scene unfolded at the Triangle factory. For more than an hour she and others watched helplessly as flames consumed the upper reaches of the building and terrified young girls crashed onto the pavement eight or nine stories below, their blood spraying the surrounding area. The horrific scene remained with Perkins, and its impact drove her to seek better conditions for workers first as a member of New York State's Industrial Commission and later as Franklin D. Roosevelt's secretary of labor. She served in the national post from 1932 to 1945.

Years later she spoke about the effects of the fire on herself and on the labor movement: "Out of that terrible episode came a self-examination of stricken conscience in which the people of [New York] saw for the first time the individual worth and value of each of those 146 people who fell or were burned in that great fire. . . . Moved by this sense of stricken guilt, we banded ourselves together to find a way by law to prevent this kind of disaster." In the wake of the tragedy, the owners of the factory were prosecuted for manslaughter, but the jury found them not guilty. They agreed to settle twenty-three civil suits in 1914 by paying $75 for each victim represented in the court cases.

FRICTION BETWEEN LABOR AND COMPANIES

Many people who opposed unions held the paternalistic view expressed by George Frederick Baer, president of the Philadelphia and Reading Railroad Company, that it was up to business owners to care for their workers. "The rights and interests of the laboring man will be protected and cared for, not by the labor agitators, but by the Christian men to whom God in his infinite wisdom has given control of the property interests of the country," Baer told a Cleveland newspaper reporter in the early 1900s.

The Triangle factory fire, however, showed that owners did not necessarily fulfill their responsibility to workers. Outrage over the incident increased the public's support of unions and helped persuade more workers to join. By 1914 membership in unions had risen to almost 2.7 million. Nevertheless, the vast majority of unskilled workers remained unprotected by unions.

The growth in union membership alarmed employers, who turned to their own national organizations to fight the trend. The National Association of Manufacturers (NAM), the National Metal Trades Association, the American Anti-Boycott Association, the Citizens' Industrial Association, and the National Founders Association spearheaded an effort to preserve the right of employers to hire nonunion workers. By hiring workers who were not union members, business owners could weaken unions and reduce their finances.

Unions favored a closed shop, which required all workers to join the union before they could be hired. They argued that since all workers benefited from wage increases and better working conditions won by the union, all should support the union by being members and paying dues. Allowing workers not to join the union, they said, undermined the union's ability to negotiate contracts and gave employers a way to pit workers against each other.

The manufacturers' groups launched a national campaign to turn the public against unions. National ads proclaimed

Americans should have "the right to work" and advocated laws that put more limits on unions. The successful strategy yielded new "right-to-work" laws that banned closed shops in many areas. The organizations also put union activists on blacklists, preventing them from being hired, and offered aid to companies involved in labor disputes. As a result, union membership stagnated for the next several years.

The courts also played a role in restricting unions, although at times rulings contradicted each other. The Supreme Court issued several rulings that stopped unions from organizing and levied fines on unions and their members. In cases in 1922 and 1925 involving a labor dispute at an Arkansas mine in which nonunion workers were killed and property damaged, the Court issued rulings at odds with each other. In the first case, *United Mine Workers* v. *Coronado Coal Company*, the Court ruled that because the mining operation was local and crossed no state lines, the Sherman AntiTrust Act did not apply. But when the mine owners appealed, the Court reversed its earlier stance and declared that the union intended to restrain interstate trade when it went on strike, and therefore the strike was illegal under the antitrust law.

When the UMW attempted to unionize mines in West Virginia, state courts used the latter Coronado case to stop the effort. The Supreme Court denied the union's appeal, letting stand the lower court's ruling that the UMW had participated in a "conspiracy in restraint of trade." The Clayton Act, an amendment to the Sherman Act passed in 1914, specifically allowed workers to picket peacefully. The Supreme Court upheld that right in a 1921 decision, but the ruling also gave the courts the power to limit the number of pickets allowed at a site. Another case that year, *Truax* v. *Corrigan*, struck down an Arizona law that permitted picketing as long as it was peaceful. A later Court decision, however, upheld a similar law in Wisconsin.

Companies had little incentive to negotiate with unions when they could take them to court. Even when companies lost the case, the long delay and the expensive court proceedings usually caused unions to give up the fight. The confusing and contradictory laws and court rulings encouraged both sides to ignore regulations and turn to violence to win their point. Employers kept "black lists" of union activists and refused to hire anyone who had union ties, paid workers to spy on union leaders, and replaced union workers with nonunion laborers. They threw out already-approved union contracts and instead adopted "yellow-dog" agreements with workers who agreed not to join a union as a condition of hiring. Union members attacked "scabs," nonunion workers brought in by the company to take the place of strikers. When tensions flared, strikers damaged buildings and other property and threatened managers and company executives. Both sides used coercion to pressure workers to vote for or against the formation of a union.

SUPPORT FOR COLLECTIVE BARGAINING

The entrance of the United States into World War I in 1917 created a shortage of workers, giving unions more leverage. Manufacturers struggled to keep up with orders for war-related products. Strikes would have caused a serious slowdown in production, which businesses and the government wanted to avoid. Employers became more willing to negotiate with unions, and the government set up several organizations to mediate labor disputes. The War Labor Board, formed in 1918, set standards that both protected unions and hindered their growth. Under the board's rules, unions had the right to represent workers and to negotiate on their behalf. Companies that had previously had closed shops were required to continue hiring only union workers. In turn, unions could not require the hiring of union workers at companies that currently had open shops.

The increase in production during the war and a pent-up demand for consumer goods after it ended led to a booming economy. Businesses prospered, but they did not willingly share the wealth with workers. The cost of living rose, while the relative value of wages declined. Once released from wartime regulations, many companies resumed their prewar resistance to unions and union contracts. Workers increasingly turned to unions to demand their fair share of the nation's prosperity. In 1920, two years after the war ended, union members numbered well over five million. Nearly one-fifth of workers in nonagricultural jobs belonged to a union.

The 1920s also marked the formation of multinational companies and the introduction of mass production of consumer goods. The use of technology allowed companies to eliminate a number of jobs held by skilled workers. Hiring lower-paid unskilled workers to operate the machines, manufacturers began producing more goods with fewer workers for greater profits. With money at hand, some of these giant companies took steps that wooed employees away from the unions. The corporations increased wages and improved working conditions, demonstrating to workers that they no longer needed to pay union dues for benefits that the company would provide anyway.

Some companies also set up their own boards to deal with worker complaints. By doing so, they gave workers a way to settle disputes through the company rather than through unions. The arrangement also served to increase the workers' loyalty to the company. These programs plus new efforts by employers to hire nonunion workers, break strikes, and serve injunctions against unions led to a decline in union membership in the mid– and late–1920s.

There was one ray of hope for unions in 1926. That year Congress passed the Railway Labor Act, which focused on avoiding labor disputes by requiring employers and unions to reach terms satisfactory to both sides through collective bargaining. The law gave official status to union negotiators and stipulated that both unions and employers select their own members of the bargaining team "without interference, influence or coercion." In 1930 the Supreme Court unanimously upheld the law and overturned the *Adair* ruling of 1908. The decision in the case, *Texas & New Orleans Railroad Company* v. *Brotherhood of Railway & Steamship Clerks*, barred the railroad from firing workers who refused to quit their own union and join the one set up by the company. It was considered one of the Court's most liberal decisions in a labor-related case.

THE GREAT DEPRESSION

Before the decade ended, the economy had plummeted into the worst economic morass the nation had ever experienced. The credit that had helped build the boom times collapsed, and the nation's economy headed into a downward spiral that would not hit bottom until 1941 when America entered World War II. During the Great Depression, as it became known, unions faced new losses. By 1933 nearly sixteen million Americans were out of work, and union membership had dipped to less than three million.

Nevertheless, the Depression helped turn the tide against the big corporations, which the American public blamed in

part for the economic disaster, and toward unions as representatives of workers. Government leaders saw the folly in
allowing one entity, the corporations, to have so much control while workers had so little. To help balance the power
between worker and employer, Congress passed the Norris–
La Guardia Anti-Injunction Act in 1932. Republicans led the
effort to pass the bill. The law severely limited courts from
issuing orders against strikes and other union actions.

For the first time, the U.S. government officially adopted a
labor policy that supported the right of workers to join a union
without harassment from employers. The act acknowledged
that the government had helped protect owners' property
and their right to form associations and set up corporations,
while "helpless" workers had no similar ability to make contracts for themselves or to protect the terms of their labor.
In no uncertain terms, the act affirmed that every worker
should have "full freedom of association, self-organization,
and designation of representatives of his own choosing, to
negotiate the terms and conditions of his employment," and
that workers should "be free from the interference, restraint,
or coercion of employers" when doing so.

Passage of the act freed unions from the constant barrage
of injunctions that in the past had interfered with their ability to strike, picket, boycott, and take other actions to bolster
their position. Under the new law, injunctions would apply
only to violent acts. In addition, the act required proof of an
individual's guilt in illegal acts; no longer could unions or
their members be held responsible for the actions of individual lawbreakers. The new law also required employers to
honor union contracts and voided any "yellow-dog" agreements made with workers who had been hired only after
they pledged not to join a union.

Unemployed workers huddle next to a Christmas tree that adorns their shack on East 12th Street, New York City, in 1938. Many people lost their jobs during the Depression, which began in 1929 and lasted more than ten years. The National Industrial Recovery Act was one of many strategies employed by the administration of President Franklin D. Roosevelt to ease unemployment and resolve labor problems.

CHAPTER THREE

Passage of the Wagner Act

The election of 1932 brought Franklin D. Roosevelt and a new Democratic Congress to power. They determined to lift the country out of depression and bring it back to economic health. Congress passed a major initiative, the National Industrial Recovery Act (NIRA), which became law on June 16, 1933. The act had three protections for workers:

1) workers had the right to organize unions and negotiate the terms of employment through collective bargaining;

2) employers could not require workers to join company unions or pledge not to join labor unions as a condition of employment;

3) employers had to abide by standards set by the president regarding minimum wage, maximum hours of labor, and other work conditions.

With the law's enactment, union membership again began to increase. But so, too, did membership in so-called company unions. Employers set up these groups to act as a substitute for trade unions. The company unions were supposed to represent workers, but without the independence of trade unions, they almost always followed the company line. While some resolved individual complaints, most of these organizations generally favored the company position over one that benefited workers. Despite the law's prohibitions, employers sometimes coerced workers into joining company unions to prevent them from setting up trade unions of their own.

Employers continued to resist the existence of unions, and workers went on strike when collective bargaining failed to resolve labor disputes. The Roosevelt administration, struggling to get the economy back on track, recognized the need to settle such disputes before strikes disrupted business. In August 1933 the president set up a National Labor Board to settle conflicts between employers and workers and ensure that strikes or other work stoppages did not interfere with the nation's economic recovery. The board also oversaw compliance by companies and unions of the Anti-Injunction Act of 1932. Senator Robert F. Wagner, a Democrat from New York, served as the labor board's chairman. The board was later replaced with the National Labor Relations Board, established on June 29, 1934.

The NIRA undertook a massive restructuring of the nation's economy and the way companies did business. Putting antitrust laws on hold, the NIRA required businesses to form alliances and set standards for all companies within an industry. These new codes set quotas on production, fixed prices and wages, and put other restrictions on companies. For example, the textile industry became among the first to set a minimum wage for textile workers and a maximum number of hours to be worked during a day. Roosevelt created the National Recovery Administration (NRA) to oversee

The members of the National Labor Board gather on January 31, 1933. The board arbitrated labor disputes. Senator Robert F. Wagner is seated in center.

the program. Firms that voluntarily adopted the codes displayed NRA decals with a blue eagle emblem on their doors to demonstrate their patriotism. The radical new program immediately sparked controversy. Business leaders, labor leaders, and many others attacked the plan. In 1935 the U.S. Supreme Court, in *Schechter Poultry Corporation* v. *United States*, struck down the NIRA as unconstitutional.

In the wake of the ruling, there seemed no way to resolve the labor disputes that continued to arise. Senator Wagner's solution lay in a bill he introduced in February 1935. The legislation had a name almost as unwieldy as the problems it sought to resolve: "A Bill to Promote Equality of Bargaining Power between Employers and Employees, to Diminish the Causes of Labor Disputes . . . and for Other Purposes." The name was shortened to the National Labor Relations Act of 1935. It later became known as the Wagner Act, for the senator who first proposed it. Among other things, the bill proposed a permanent National Labor Relations Board (NLRB) to oversee dealings between employers and workers and their unions.

At hearings held by the Senate Committee on Education and Labor the following March and April, the U.S. Chamber of Commerce and the National Association of Manufacturers, as well as other industry groups, volleyed a barrage of criticism at Wagner's bill. Despite industry's fierce opposition, the Senate committee voted unanimously for the bill. It met with little criticism from the full Senate when it reached the floor. Senator Millard E. Tydings, a Democrat from Maryland, proposed an amendment that would have barred both unions and employers (and anyone else) from using coercion. The measure failed on a 21 to 50 vote, and the Senate approved the original bill, 63 to 12, after only two days of debate.

The House was still considering the bill when the Supreme Court ruled in the *Schechter* case, putting an end to Roosevelt's National Recovery Act on the grounds that it was unconstitutional. As a result of the Court ruling, House members changed the labor bill's focus slightly to "promote industrial peace" by removing obstacles to workers' ability to unionize. Again, industry spokesmen went all out to defeat the bill. Industrialists testified at hearings of the House Committee on Labor that the legislation threatened owners' rights to property and to conduct their business as they saw fit. They pressed for an amendment, again unsuccessfully, that would have required unions as well as employers to refrain from coercion.

While many business leaders adamantly opposed the Wagner bill, the majority of Americans favored the legislation. Polls conducted throughout this period showed an overwhelming support for the bill among the nation's voters.

They believed that workers had the right to better wages and conditions and that government should protect that right.

The full House spent a day debating the legislation, then passed it without a recorded vote. At conference, the House and the Senate agreed to minor changes in the final bill, which President Roosevelt signed on July 5, 1935.

NEW POLICIES, NEW PROTECTIONS

The Wagner Act represented a radical new government policy that saw unions as a tool to ensure the peaceful "free flow of commerce." The act regulated all private industries involved in interstate trade, with the exception of railroads and airlines. It did not cover government employees, farm workers, supervisors, and those conducting business only in one state. For the first time, the government provided real protection for unions against employers who interfered with their right to organize and bargain for the workers they represented.

Employers' refusal to allow unions to negotiate for workers inevitably led to strikes, work stoppages, and other actions that interfered with business. Protecting the unions' right to negotiate work conditions, Congress believed, would help ease the tensions that often led to strikes. Employers, no longer able to ignore unions or to rely on friendly courts to grant injunctions, would be more willing to use mediation and other cooperative methods to resolve disputes.

The act also aimed to keep wages stable and more competitive. As a result, the law's supporters said, workers would spend more, which would ultimately lift the overall economy and help keep it on an even keel.

The act barred employers from:

- interfering with or coercing employees who exercised their rights as guaranteed by law;

• interfering with efforts to form or run a union or play any role in a union (contributing money or supporting it in other ways);

• discriminating against workers or prospective workers to encourage or discourage union membership. When workers voted to have a closed shop, however, employers were required to hire union members.

• taking measures against employees who filed charges against the company or testified about violations to the act;

• refusing to negotiate with a legitimate union representative.

The act also established the National Labor Relations Board to take the place of the National Labor Board. Among its responsibilities, the new board investigated complaints, held hearings, and issued decisions and orders based on the findings. The board could enforce its orders by filing a petition against violators in the circuit court of appeals. Employers or workers who disputed a board decision could also seek redress in the circuit court.

Because of the adversarial nature of its duties, the NLRB almost immediately became embroiled in controversy. Industry continued its assault on the new law that created the board and filed a number of suits challenging the act's constitutionality. The most important case was *National Labor Relations Board* v. *Jones & Laughlin Steel Corporation.*

The U.S. Constitution, in Article I, section 8, gave Congress the power to "regulate Commerce . . . among the several states." Congress invoked that power when it passed the Wagner Act, which gave authority to a federal board to oversee labor relations in companies that participated in interstate commerce. For years the U.S. Supreme Court had rejected laws based on Congress's power to regulate interstate commerce. In the *Jones and Laughlin* case, however, the Court reversed course and ruled in favor of the Wagner Act and the NLRB.

The case involved a labor dispute between the union of ironworkers, steelworkers, and tinworkers and the Jones & Laughlin Steel Corporation in Aliquippa, Pennsylvania. The union filed a complaint with the NLRB alleging that the company was discriminating against workers who wanted to join the union and had fired some of the organizers. After reviewing the case, the NLRB ruled in favor of the union and ordered the company to stop its unfair labor practices. When Jones & Laughlin appealed to the federal circuit court of appeals and won, the NLRB took the case to the U.S. Supreme Court.

The company argued that it did business only within the state and therefore Congress had no power to control its dealings with employees. Federal officials contended that labor disputes in steel companies, even those operating only within a state, had a significant impact on interstate commerce. In April 1937 the Supreme Court, in a 5 to 4 decision, ruled that Congress did have the power to enact the Wagner Act and that the law was constitutional. Chief Justice Charles Evans Hughes, who wrote the majority opinion for the Court, noted that Congress had the power to protect interstate commerce from all manner of dangers. That included strikes and other actions arising from labor unrest. Even labor disputes within a state had the potential of affecting the steel industry and trade between states, the Court concluded.

Chief Justice Hughes recognized the right of workers to form unions: "Employees have as clear a right to organize and select their representatives for lawful purposes as [a company] has to organize its business and select its own officers and agents." He repeated the Court's previous assessment that unions were "essential to give laborers opportunity to deal on an [equal basis] with their employer." The decision marked a major milestone for the act and the future of unions. It also signaled that the Court would allow Congress more power to regulate entities under the Constitution's commerce clause.

With the legality of the Wagner Act assured by the Court, five states enacted similar legislation. New York, Wisconsin, Massachusetts, Pennsylvania, and Utah all passed laws in 1937 to protect the right of unions and workers. Many more states, however, began to adopt laws that restricted union activity. Two years later Wisconsin and Pennsylvania joined other states in passing new laws which regulated both union and industry actions.

When the constitutionality issue failed to dismantle the Wagner Act, industry tried other tactics to crush unions. Some 2,500 businesses, including some of the largest corporations in the country, ignored the law and waged an underground battle against unions. According to the report of the Senate's Civil Liberties Committee, released in December 1937, the companies hired nearly four thousand agents over a four-year period to spy on unions, stir up antiunion sentiment among employees, and undermine union elections. The firms also hired thugs to beat up union organizers, threaten prounion workers, and break up strikes. In addition the committee revealed that many of the corporations had stockpiled weapons to deal with prounion activity. The Republic Steel Company, for example, spent $79,000 on tear gas and other chemicals; the Youngstown Sheet and Tube

Company purchased eight machine guns, 369 rifles, 190 shotguns, and 450 revolvers. Industrial espionage, the committee concluded, allowed "private corporations [to] dominate their employees, deny them their constitutional rights, promote disorder and disharmony, and [nullify] the powers of the government itself."

The committee uncovered a less-violent but just as effective strategy developed by the companies to discredit unions and their leaders. The method, devised during a strike at the Remington Rand plant in New York's Mohawk Valley region in 1936, played on townspeople's fears to turn them against the union. During the Mohawk Valley strike, company officials spread rumors that the union's leaders were outside agitators and subversives who posed a danger to the community's law and order. The company persuaded local police to break up strikes and union meetings and intimidated other workers to vote against unions. Remington's owners also used economic pressure, threatening to move the business to another town if local leaders did not support the company's antiunion position. This strategy, which became known as the Mohawk Valley Formula, served as a blueprint for firms aiming to derail union activities. The revelations of the committee report elicited public disgust at such tactics. Despite the criticism, however, many companies adopted the "scientific method" of strikebreaking used in Mohawk Valley.

MORE SUPPORT FOR WORKERS

The Supreme Court's ruling that the Wagner Act was constitutional gave President Roosevelt the assurance he needed to address minimum wages and maximum hours for workers again. He proposed the Fair Labor Standards bill in May 1937, a month after the Supreme Court's decision. The bill

In early 1937 Labor Secretary Frances Perkins (*center*) discusses the Fair Labor Standards bill, which she endorsed, with Senator Hugo L. Black (*left*) of Alabama (later Supreme Court justice) and Representative William P. Connery Jr., (*right*) a Democrat from Massachusetts who chaired the House Labor Committee.

encompassed several of the original NRA standards, including minimum wages, a shorter work week, and the abolition of child labor. An unimpressed Congress relegated the bill to committee. When the lawmakers convened without taking action on the legislation, Roosevelt called a special session in November to force Congress to address the issue. Even labor gave the bill lukewarm support. William Green, head of the AFL, opposed minimum wage requirements, which he feared would encourage businesses to pay no more than the standard. Business groups argued against the legislation, but for opposite reasons.

Under pressure from the Roosevelt administration and with the public's blessing, Congress finally passed an amended version of the bill in June 1938. As enacted, the law set a 25-cent-an-hour minimum wage, which would increase to

40 cents an hour over seven years; established a work week of 44 hours, which would go to 40 hours in three years; and banned the hiring of children under sixteen by businesses involved in interstate trade. The passage of the bill represented a giant step by the government into the affairs of labor and management. With the lessons of the Depression still in front of them, the American people had abandoned the earlier philosophy that companies should be left alone to do whatever they wished.

The courts, too, began to shift away from the view that business regulations were necessarily unconstitutional. In a 1937 case that tested the constitutionality of the new standards, the Supreme Court gave the constitutional green light to "regulation which is reasonable in relation to its subject and is adopted in the interests of the community." Following that ruling, in *West Coast Hotel Company* v. *Parrish*, the Court issued a number of decisions that allowed unions to bypass the antitrust laws and gave workers the right to strike, walk picket lines, and organize boycotts.

In the 1938 *NLRB* v. *Mackay Radio* case, however, the Supreme Court weighed in on the side of management. The Court ruled that employers had the right to hire permanent workers to replace strikers. In the decision, the Court decreed that such hirings were not barred by the Wagner Act's prohibition against anything that might "interfere with or impede or diminish in any way the right to strike." Pro-labor critics argued that the *Mackay* ruling severely damaged the effectiveness of workers' strikes.

To some, however, the Supreme Court's rulings tipped the balance too far in favor of unions. Businesses, in particular, agreed with Justice Robert H. Jackson's dissent in a boycott case that unions had won "the same arbitrary dominance

Incidents like the one shown here of striking Teamsters battling police in Minneapolis in 1934 gave unions a bad name among the American public.

over the economic sphere . . . that labor so long, so bitterly and so rightly asserted should belong to no man."

Despite the gains made by labor, many employers continued to resist unions by punishing prounion workers and refusing to participate in collective bargaining. Labor unrest and strikes over these issues plagued the nation during much of the 1930s. These disturbances began to whittle away public support for unions and government regulations that favored workers. At the end of 1933 some four million workers belonged to the American Federation of Labor, the largest labor association. By 1935, however, membership in all unions had fallen below the four million mark.

President Roosevelt clung to his belief that strong unions and good working conditions benefited the entire society. Collective bargaining, which gave unions the ability to forge contracts for their members, "must remain as the foundation of industrial relations for all time," Roosevelt asserted.

CHAPTER FOUR

Union Growth and World War II

By 1933 industrial workers accounted for the largest growth in union membership. Rather than joining unions based on a particular job, mass production workers set up unions to cover whole industries. These industrial unions wanted equal representation in the American Federation of Labor. But the craft unions fought to retain control of the organization. They set up a system that divided members of industrial unions into existing craft unions.

More moderate leaders in the AFL argued that the organization should accept the industrial unions on an equal footing with the old-time craft unions. John L. Lewis, the dynamic president of the United Mine Workers, led the campaign to accept the industrial unions. A shrewd and powerful figure who had gone to work in the coal pits of Iowa at the age of twelve, Lewis had earned a national reputation as a union organizer after building UMW membership from 150,000 to 400,000 in the early 1930s.

The battle over industrial unions soon developed into a power struggle between AFL's president, William Green, and Lewis. A compromise worked out at the AFL convention in 1934 pledged to give industrial unions some power within the organization. When AFL leaders failed to deliver on the promises, however, Lewis and his supporters demanded that the federation change its policies. At the next year's convention, Lewis blamed the AFL's rules for undermining the new industrial unions, which, the UMW chief said, were "dying like the grass withering before the autumn sun." When the AFL delegates refused to change their ways, the fiery Lewis and his followers formed an advisory board, which they called the Committee for Industrial Organization.

Angry AFL leaders demanded that the group disband. Lewis ignored the edict, resigned as AFL vice president, and redoubled his efforts to win support for industrial unions. By the summer of 1936 the committee had attracted ten AFL unions to its cause. Green and the other members of the executive council suspended the unions' AFL membership. More moderate labor leaders feared that the widening rift would weaken the labor movement. They urged that the two organizations join forces and present a united front against management. At the end of 1937 leaders of the two organizations met and discussed proposals for a merger. But by then the Committee for Industrial Organization represented some 3.7 million workers from thirty-two unions compared to 3.4 million workers affiliated with the AFL. Neither leader wanted to relinquish power to join in a united federation.

The committee, which became the Congress for Industrial Organization (CIO), operated similarly to the AFL in setting up a national association. The CIO's first great success was in the steel industry. In just six months in 1936 the CIO set up the Steel Workers' Organizing Committee (SWOC) and attracted more than 100,000 members to the union. The steel industry, which had long opposed unions, did its best to thwart the effort. Company owners placed full-page ads in newspapers around the country charging that the unionists were Communists who wanted to take over the country's economic system. In the end, however, the owners conceded defeat as workers overwhelmingly signed up with the SWOC (later the United Steelworkers of America).

Taking advantage of the astounding success of the membership campaign, CIO's Lewis secretly negotiated a pact with U.S. Steel Corporation, once the world's largest corporation and America's biggest steel company. Aware that the union could call a strike that would disrupt the entire industry, the corporation agreed to Lewis's demands for an eight-hour day, forty-hour workweek, with a 10 percent increase in wages and extra pay for overtime work. U.S. Steel (often referred to as "Big Steel") also agreed to deal with the SWOC union as the legitimate negotiator for workers. Both sides agreed to binding arbitration to settle disputes.

There were several reasons for the SWOC's quick success: a majority of Big Steel's workers were already union members, and the union had the political backing of the governor of Pennsylvania as well as several leaders in Congress; U.S. Steel did not want a labor dispute to disrupt production just as demand for steel was rising rapidly; and the company wanted to avoid a strike that could jeopardize lucrative contracts with the British for armaments as that nation prepared for war. In the end, officials at U.S. Steel recognized that accepting the union made the most financial sense, and that the company would have to abandon the old line of fierce resistance to unions held by some other industry chiefs.

From left, Philip Murray, SWOC chairman; Lee Pressman, CIO attorney; R. J. Thomas, UAW vice president; Homer Martin, UAW president; John L. Lewis, CIO president; and John Brophy, CIO director, meet in 1938 to settle a factional dispute over union representation.

The pact represented a landmark in the history of labor relations. The company's acknowledgment of unions' power would set the course for other major industries in their dealings with workers and the unions that represented them.

MEMORIAL DAY MASSACRE

Republic Steel, Inland Steel, and other steel companies, known as "Little Steel" because they were smaller than the giant U.S. Steel, continued to resist the union's push. Fewer of the workers employed by the smaller companies were members of the union. Fierce in their opposition to unions, the officers of these companies resorted to violence to crush strikes and other union activity. In May 1937 SWOC led a strike against three of the steel firms after company executives refused to sign contracts with the union. Most of the steel plants closed during the strike, but Republic continued production at its South Chicago factory. Police barred workers from picketing in front of Republic's property, despite the Wagner Act's protection of such action and the mayor's assurances that the city would allow peaceful picketing.

Police and strikers tussled outside the plant gates for several days. The *New York Times* reported that on May 29 union strikers, "armed with baseball bats and clubs," began a siege that injured eighteen protesters and six policemen. The article noted that "loyal Republic employees" had asked the mayor to close down the picket line and allow them to return to work. Union leaders charged that the police force was "being used as a common strike-breaking agency by the steel corporation."

The next afternoon, on Memorial Day, hundreds of steelworkers and their supporters, including women and children, gathered in Chicago near the Republic Steel plant. As the group began to make its way toward the steel mill, armed police called by the factory owner met them and refused to let the marchers set up a picket line. Tension mounted during the standoff. Suddenly a protester threw a stick at the police line. In the melee that followed, police threw tear gas bombs, and more sticks were hurled at officers. One officer fired a revolver into the air. As the marchers ran away from the gunfire, other officers took aim and fired into the crowd. Mollie West, a member of the Typographical Union Local 16 who joined the steelworkers' demonstration, later recalled a police officer's warning to her, "Get off the field, or I'll put a bullet in your back." She ran.

After firing off two hundred rounds, the police switched to billy clubs and beat any marcher in their path. Officers herded protesters still on the scene into paddy wagons and

Police wielding guns, clubs, and tear gas canisters attack strikers outside Chicago's Republic Steel plant on May 30, 1937, during a labor dispute.

threw the wounded in on top of them. Ten marchers died of gunshot wounds that day; another eighty-eight required medical treatment for their injuries, including thirty who had been shot. Thirty-five officers received care for minor injuries; three spent the night in the hospital.

Local residents staged a protest over the police handling of the Memorial Day Massacre, as the riot came to be known. Many other Americans, however, blamed the union for the violence. The *Chicago Tribune*, which typically sided with management in its coverage, reported that the strikers, armed with guns, were Communist Party members who had planned to take over the steel plant and remove nonunion workers.

A Senate committee formed to investigate the Memorial Day violence exonerated the union. Issued the following

December, the report concluded that the workers had a right to picket peacefully in front of the plant and that had been the marchers' intention. The report determined that the police, not the strikers, had been the ones to use excessive force and that the officers could have avoided the violence that erupted.

In the aftermath of the massacre, union officials eventually called off the strike. Ultimately, the union won its battle with Little Steel after filing a complaint with the National Labor Relations Board. It took four years, but in 1941, the companies agreed to stop unfair labor practices and negotiated contracts with the steel union a year later. In addition, the NLRB agreement required Republic Steel to reinstate hundreds of workers fired during the 1937 strike and distribute tens of thousands of dollars in back pay.

UNIONIZATION OF AUTO PLANTS

Also in the 1930s workers at automobile plants throughout the nation began to form unions and negotiate contracts. By 1936 most of the small auto unions had joined the United Automobile Workers (UAW), which in turn became a member of the CIO. The UAW became a symbol of union strength when its members staged a sit-down strike in early 1937 and shut down operations at General Motors (GM), at that time the largest manufacturing company in the world. During the six-week strike at four GM plants, Michigan governor Frank Murphy mobilized the national guard to keep the peace. The governor, Secretary of Labor Frances Perkins, and President Roosevelt helped forge an agreement between the union and the automobile manufacturer. The settlement ended the strike and gave the UAW the right to negotiate contracts on behalf of GM's union workers in the future.

The GM settlement sparked the establishment of unions at other automobile plants. By spring 1937 all the major U.S. car companies except Ford had signed union contracts. Henry Ford, a longtime foe of unions, defied the Wagner Act and declared that his company would "never recognize the United Auto Workers Union or any other union." Labor unions, Ford said, were "the worst thing that ever struck the earth because they take away a man's independence."

On May 26, 1937, about fifty UAW representatives tried to distribute pamphlets to workers at Ford's Dearborn plant. The union men and women gathered at the plant entrance near an overpass that allowed workers to cross over the road to get to work. As news reporters and photographers watched, men hired by the company's service center attacked the union organizers. The attackers, including a professional boxer, two wrestlers, and members of a local gang, punched and kicked the unionists.

Walter P. Reuther, later to become UAW president, suffered major injuries when the attackers threw him down the overpass steps and kicked him. One man broke his back, another was kicked in the head and groin, and several women sustained injuries during the affair. Reports of the attack, dubbed the Battle of the Overpass, and photographs of the battered unionists, circulated in newspapers nationwide. The incident became a rallying point for labor unions everywhere.

Following the attack, the National Labor Relations Board ordered Ford to stop interfering with union efforts. Ford appealed the NLRB ruling and granted two wage hikes in hopes of convincing workers that a union was unnecessary. Company spies continued to report on union activity, and workers lived in fear of violence from antiunion officials. Despite the company's efforts, the union slowly began to win support among Ford workers. On April 2, 1941, work-ers went on strike at the Dearborn factory. Ford agreed to let them vote on union membership if they called off the strike. The elections, held May 21, astounded Ford, who had underestimated the union's strength among workers. Only 2.6 percent voted against a union. A large majority of work-ers voted to join the UAW rather than the AFL affiliate, also on the ballot. Ford, who had lost several battles in court and faced an NLRB hearing on charges of violence and racketeer-ing, agreed to a UAW contract that included an industry-high wage, a union shop, and seniority for employees.

NLRB UNDER FIRE

By the end of the 1930s, more than eight million workers belonged to unions. Continuing friction between the two national labor organizations, however, undercut the move-ment's effectiveness. AFL leaders characterized the CIO as a Communist front, while CIO officers charged that the AFL was operating as a tool of management. Such attacks tainted the public's view of all unions.

Both labor organizations had expanded membership to include skilled and unskilled workers. Problems arose when an AFL union overlapped with a CIO union. In some cases, one group's union organized workers only to be stymied when the other group's union signed an agreement with management giving it the authority to negotiate for workers. Battles over jurisdiction erupted. These disputes, which sometimes led to strikes, weakened labor's cause. The strikes interrupted business and interfered with customer orders, which further alienated industry and angered the public.

The rancor between the groups also affected the National Labor Relations Board. The NLRB found itself in the middle of disputes over which union should represent workers. Regardless of the outcome of a decision, the losing side heaped criticism on the board. The fact that labor as well as management found fault with the NLRB helped undermine the public's confidence in the board's work.

As the number of unions and union members rose in the late 1930s and 1940s, the mountain of complaints the board had to investigate grew dramatically. The entrance of the United States into World War II in 1941 posed additional problems for the board, which Roosevelt put in charge of war labor disputes. This increased the board's workload even more. Understaffed, inexperienced, and underfunded, the three-member NLRB soon accumulated a huge backlog of cases. Its inability to deal quickly with cases stirred further criticism of the board.

Despite the difficulties it faced, the NLRB had a good record of resolving disputes and winning court approval of a majority of the cases it heard. During its twelve years in operation under the Wagner Act, the board resolved more than 100,000 cases, most handled through mediation or other informal methods without the need of a formal edict. Over the same period of time, circuit courts set aside only 12.6 percent of the board's decisions.

The board's activities had a marked effect on workers and unions. In the last nine years of the Wagner Act (1938 to 1947), as a direct result of NLRB orders, employers were forced to reinstate more than 76,000 workers who had been illegally fired because of union activities. Companies also had to rehire more than 226,000 strikers and issue back pay of nearly $12.5 million to 40,691 workers. As part of the settlements, the companies had to post notices at the workplace informing employees that they would not be discriminated against for joining a union or participating in union activities. The Wagner board conducted almost 37,000 union elections during its existence, and workers voted in favor of unions more than 80 percent of the time.

Over the course of the board's existence, the number of workers in unions more than tripled. By 1946 between 80 percent and nearly 100 percent of the workforce at many of the nation's largest industries belonged to unions.

LABOR IN THE POLITICAL ARENA

As the labor organizations increased in strength, their influence on politics and political campaigns grew. During the 1936 presidential campaign, both the AFL and the CIO supported President Roosevelt's bid for reelection. "Labor has gained more under President Roosevelt than under any president in memory," CIO's Lewis said. "Obviously it is the duty of labor to support Roosevelt 100 per cent in the next election." Other Democrats benefited from labor support as well. The party had proved its worth to labor by promoting the prolabor programs of the New Deal.

Roosevelt's victory, won with the help of union members, spurred labor's opponents into action. Alarmed at the growing influence of unions on the nation's politics, they embarked on a campaign to discredit the labor movement. The effort focused on the presence of Communists among the leaders of the labor movement, particularly the CIO. American Communists and socialists were among many groups working to strengthen the unions. The National Association of Manufacturers and other business lobbyists charged that Communists had seized control of the unions. One antiunion pamphlet distributed to workers read "Join the C.I.O. and Help Build a Soviet America."

In the late 1930s, Communists controlled Russia and several other East European countries that formed the Union of Soviet Socialist Republics (USSR). Communism, as espoused by Karl Marx in his 1848 book *The Communist Manifesto*, appealed to some in the American labor movement. They embraced Marx's view of a classless society in which workers shared in the fruits of their labor. Many other Americans, however, feared that Communism would eradicate individual liberties. These people distrusted American Communists and believed, often without justification, that their loyalties lay with the USSR rather than with the United States.

In 1939 Adolf Hitler's Germany invaded Poland, triggering the start of World War II in Europe. The events set off a war of words in the United States. One faction, including CIO's Lewis, aviator hero Charles Lindbergh, and the American Communist Party, among others, wanted to keep out of the war. Another group, including most other labor leaders, believed America should not enter the war as combatants but supported Roosevelt's view that the United States should provide aid to England and other European allies.

Lewis, no longer Roosevelt's champion, urged his followers to vote for the Republican presidential candidate, Wendell Willkie, in the 1940 election and pledged to step down as CIO head if union members disregarded his advice. Roosevelt won election to an unprecedented third term, thanks in part to overwhelming support from the labor vote. True to his word, Lewis resigned as CIO president but retained his post as leader of the UMW.

LEADING UP TO WAR

By 1941 Americans had become increasingly uneasy over the expanding war abroad and supported efforts to improve U.S.

defense systems. Unions pledged to do their part to protect America and provide war materiel for the allies. But they also wanted to make sure that workers as well as owners benefited from the profits reaped in the improving economy.

Antiunion forces grabbed the opportunity to discredit unions and to circumvent requirements that benefited workers. They labeled any strike or worker protest as unpatriotic. Companies illegally ignored unions' demands for collective bargaining, claiming they were only trying to prevent work stoppages that could put the nation at risk.

Irresponsible union leaders and members further tarnished the cause of labor in the public's eyes. Newspapers featured reports on fights between unions, unreasonable demands for excessive wages, and cases of graft and corruption in unions. At businesses with closed shops, all workers had to belong to the union and any employee who did not pay dues or violated other union rules could be fired. Some unions prevented employers from firing workers who received a paycheck but did little work. This practice, known as featherbedding, drew criticism as an example of union abuse of the system.

Americans became alarmed when labor disputes affected defense-related industries. Labor unrest in 1941 resulted in a near-record number of strikes and other work actions. That year more than two million workers took part in 4,288 strikes. In March 1941 President Roosevelt set up the National Defense Mediation Board to try to avert further strikes. The board's mission was to forge labor agreements between unions and companies involved in the defense industry before a strike was called. The panel succeeded in averting some actions, but a strike by Lewis's UMW proved beyond its powers.

The miners went on strike in September when the steel industry's coal mines refused to allow union shops. Unions in other industries had successfully incorporated union shops in their contracts. In businesses with union shops, employers could hire nonunion workers but the workers had to join the union once they passed the trial period. Only about 5 percent of the mine workers did not already belong to the UMW. Miners agreed to go back to work while the mediation board reviewed the dispute, but they went out on strike again in October after the board rejected UMW's demands for union shops. In making the ruling, the board's majority declared that government should not have the power to force workers to join unions. After the board's vote, the two members who had opposed the decision, representatives of the CIO, resigned, and the CIO refused to take further disputes to the board for mediation. That spelled the end of the board, at least temporarily; it officially disbanded in January 1942 when Roosevelt replaced it with a war labor board.

The coal miners' strike posed a serious threat to steel production and the nation's defense program. Roosevelt denounced "the selfish obstruction" of the strike leaders and ordered the union to resume negotiations with the steel companies. The president declared that the government would take over the mines if necessary to ensure that the nation would continue to have steel. On November 17, after negotiations failed to produce an agreement, Lewis called for the strike to resume. After five days, Roosevelt turned the matter over to an independent three-man arbitration board to decide. The board, proposed by Lewis, consisted of the head of U.S. Steel Corporation, Lewis himself, and John R. Steelman, head of the U.S. Conciliation Service, whom Lewis knew favored union shops. Predictably, the board ruled

William Green (*right*), AFL president, presents an oil painting to President Franklin D. Roosevelt on June 10, 1941, to emphasize the union's patriotism.

for Lewis and the establishment of union shops at the coal mines. As part of the deal, the union agreed to a no-strike clause through the life of the contract, scheduled to expire March 31, 1943.

Lewis won the contract battle, but he lost ground on the public relations front. The UMW strike and others further antagonized the public, already fearful of the growing power of unions and their ability to disrupt national concerns. The president and members of Congress questioned the patriotism of workers who participated in strikes that interfered with the production of goods necessary for the nation's defense. By the end of the year twenty-two states had passed antiunion laws. Congress considered thirty bills to limit labor's power, and the House passed a measure that would have banned strikes in industries involved in defense production. Before the Senate could vote on the bill, the Imperial Japanese Navy attacked the U.S. fleet at Pearl Harbor on December 7, 1941, and the next day President Roosevelt signed a declaration of war against Japan. Three days later, the United States declared war on Germany and Italy as well.

A NATION AT WAR

The nation's entrance into World War II united Americans in a common cause. Workers joined everyone else in making sacrifices and doing whatever they could to bolster the national effort. Union leaders knew, however, they would have to keep vigilant to preserve the gains they had made under the New Deal. Roosevelt helped maintain the balance between labor and business when he appointed representatives of both to various boards overseeing wartime production and labor programs.

President Roosevelt determined to avoid strikes, which he knew could have a disastrous effect on the nation's ability to wage war effectively. In mid–December 1941 the president met with labor and business leaders to develop a program to resolve labor disputes before they disrupted production. Both sides eventually agreed to avoid strikes while the nation was at war, settle disputes before they escalated into work actions, and rely on a new federal board to settle unresolved labor disputes that could affect wartime activities. The National War Labor Board (NWLB), established by Roosevelt's executive order on January 12, 1942, had an equal number of members from the public, the unions, and business. The steelworkers' union had not yet settled its contract with the Little Steel companies when the president set up the war board. The board granted the steelworkers a raise that amounted to 15 percent overall.

When wage disputes arose in other industries, the board followed the Little Steel formula and held raises to 15 percent. However, some industries hiked wages well beyond that figure to attract scarce labor. The demand for war materiel had given the economy a needed boost in production that helped lift the nation out of the Depression of the 1930s. But spiraling costs threatened the economy anew. Prices rose as supplies dwindled; likewise, wages increased as men marched to war and the number of laborers decreased. To slow the increasing cost of living, Congress passed the Economic Stabilization Act in October 1942 at Roosevelt's request. The act gave the president the power to order controls on wages, salaries, prices, and rents, holding them to the levels on September 15, 1942. Roosevelt held the power to approve increases to further the war effort or in cases of "gross inequities."

Over the course of the war, the NWLB settled 17,650 labor disputes and authorized 415,000 wage agreements. The number of strikes and other work actions decreased dramatically during the first years of the war. Even with the board in place, however, strikes did occur during the war years. Most were settled fairly quickly. In some cases, wages could not keep pace with the rising cost of living, but the board was not able to override wage freezes ordered as part of the nation's war measures. As a compromise the board settled such disputes by proposing increases in benefits such as insurance and vacation pay. President Roosevelt intervened forty times when unions or businesses refused to agree with the board's settlement. In one such case, two members of the

U.S. Army carried the president of Montgomery Ward out of his office after he defied the board's ruling.

In April 1943 the UMW contract with coal mine operators expired. Lewis demanded an increase of $2 a day in miners' pay plus an allotment for the time miners spent underground traveling to the work site. The owners refused the terms, and the matter came before the War Labor Board. While pledging not to call a strike during wartime, Lewis nevertheless encouraged union members not to "trespass" on mining property until the contract was settled. In response to their leader's suggestion, miners left their jobs. President Roosevelt, fearing that a work stoppage would threaten the nation's war effort, seized control of the mines and ordered the miners back to work. They complied, but only because Lewis called a truce while federal officials worked on an agreement that would satisfy the union.

The press took aim at Lewis, questioning his patriotism and criticizing his unbending stand. Lewis's persistence paid off when the War Labor Board approved a raise of $1.50 a day for the miners. The controversy, however, left the public with a bad impression of Lewis and of unions in general. Fearful that other union leaders would follow Lewis's example, people began calling for laws that would prevent unions from undermining the war effort.

Congress responded by passing, over President Roosevelt's veto, the War Labor Disputes Act in June 1943. Criticized by union leaders as part of a "vicious and continuous attack on labor's rights," the law gave the president power to take over plants where strikes threatened the war effort. It also called for criminal prosecution of strike participants and organizers. Under the legislation, a thirty-day cooling off period was to be ordered for strikers at industries not involved with the

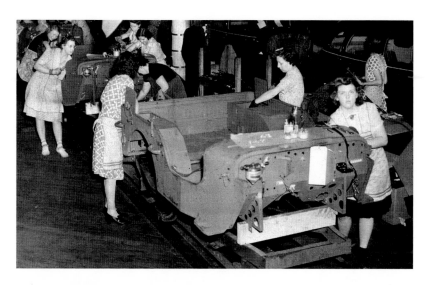

Female employees work on a jeep assembly line at a converted Willys-Overland Motors factory in Toledo, Ohio, on December 2, 1941.

war. The law also banned unions from contributing to political candidates.

Even with the law on the books, workers frustrated by low pay resorted to strikes sporadically throughout the remaining years of the war. In fall 1943, rail workers threatened to go on strike after a federal economic board rejected their negotiated wage hike. The Labor Disputes Act did not cover railroads, which were regulated under the Railway Labor Act of 1926. President Roosevelt averted a strike when he ruled the rail workers were entitled to the increased wages.

During the remaining war years workers staged a growing number of strikes to protest low wages. Half of the workers employed in manufacturing participated in strikes in 1944 and 1945. Many of these were wildcat strikes, brief work stoppages not sanctioned by unions. The war ended on August 14, 1945, with the surrender of Japan. The official truce was signed September 2.

Strikers at a Carnegie-Illinois Steel Corporation plant in Pennsylvania burn union placards in 1946 upon hearing that a new wage contract had been accepted. After the war the number of labor disputes increased.

CHAPTER FIVE

Passage of the Taft-Hartley Act

With peace at hand, both labor and management pushed for an end to the government's wage and price controls. Labor and management had voluntarily limited strikes and lockouts during the war. But the war had ended and so had their willingness to endure further restrictions. Unions were eager to seek wage hikes for their members, whose incomes had declined with the end of overtime needed for the war effort. Companies argued they could not negotiate wage increases until the government lifted price controls.

Harry S. Truman, who assumed the presidency after Roosevelt's death in April 1945, supported a return to collective bargaining to resolve wage issues. Workers, he told the American public, were entitled to wage increases "to cushion the shock [of high prices], to sustain adequate purchasing power and to raise national income." He noted, too, that businesses had reaped big profits during the war and could afford a wage increase without having to raise prices.

Enraged industry leaders immediately attacked the president. They disputed government figures showing that business profits had more than doubled during the war. If wages rose, then businesses must be able to raise prices to cover the costs, executives argued. Truman's statements prompted Senator Robert A. Taft, a Republican from Ohio and a long-time critic of the Democrats' labor policies, to remark that the president had surrendered to the CIO.

Truman turned to representatives of labor and management to find a solution. At the Labor-Management Conference of 1945, held November 5–30, the president urged both sides to find a way to resolve their differences and avert the labor strikes that threatened. He made it clear that if they did not voluntarily agree on a plan that restricted strikes, they would be faced with new laws that gave government more power to intervene.

The delegates produced good suggestions for collective bargaining procedures and the voluntary use of mediators to settle disputes. The convention ended, however, without resolving the conflict over wages and prices. The participants also failed to determine what to do in cases where collective bargaining failed and both sides did not agree to arbitration. Neither labor nor industry wanted the government to interfere with labor negotiations.

True to his word, President Truman asked Congress to pass a law that required a cooling-off period and federal fact-finding in labor disputes involving the nation's most important industries. Unions opposed the legislation because they did not want the government to restrict their ability to go on strike. Businesses spoke against the bill because they did not want to open their records to government fact finders.

RECORD NUMBER OF STRIKES

Meanwhile, several big unions had gone on strike in an effort to increase wages. During the war, employees had worked long hours and depended on overtime pay. When the war ended, demand decreased and employees worked fewer hours for less pay. Many shops laid off workers, and unemployment rolls swelled. In the fall of 1945, workers called a nationwide strike against General Motors, which lasted for 113 days and involved some 200,000 employees. A strike against General Electric went on for 58 days, and a similar work action at Westinghouse shut down production at that firm for 115 days. In January 1946, 750,000 steelworkers followed suit, staging a strike that crippled many other industries that used the metal for their products. Hundreds of smaller unions called work stoppages in shops throughout the country. As the new year began, nearly two million workers had left their jobs to demand better pay.

Faced with economic chaos, Truman set up fact-finding boards to help settle the disputes. The boards worked out increases of up to 20 percent, based on the cost of living. Companies with lower earnings were allowed to apply for price hikes to cover the higher wages granted by the boards. By spring most of the strikes had ended.

In April, UMW's Lewis demanded similar gains for his union members. When industry balked, 400,000 miners walked off their jobs. On May 21 the government took over the mines, and strikers returned to work while officials negotiated a settlement. Lewis refused to accept the government's terms and on November 21 ordered workers to resume the strike. Furious, Truman asked the district court to issue a restraining order barring the union from striking against the government. The judge called the strike "an evil, demoniac, monstrous thing," and approved the injunction. Lewis defied the court and continued the strike. He was charged with contempt of court and later found guilty and fined $10,000 personally, with a $3.5 million fine levied against the UMW. The court injunction ended the strike on December 7.

The case eventually came before the U.S. Supreme Court. Lewis and his attorneys argued that the Norris–La Guardia Act barred the court from ordering the strikers back to work. Lawyers for the federal government replied that the president's power during national emergencies overrode the act's prohibitions. While the case made its way through the legal system, Lewis and the miners' union signed a contract with the federal government that remained in force until the private owners resumed mine operation in June 1947. The contract set up a safety code for the mines and established union committees charged with overseeing workplace safety.

On March 6, 1947, the Supreme Court reduced UMW's fine to $700,000 but upheld the full amount of Lewis's fine in a 7 to 2 decision. The Court decision on whether the Norris-La Guardia Act applied was much closer. The justices agreed, by a 5 to 4 vote, that the Norris-La Guardia Act would not have permitted a court injunction if the mines had remained in the hands of the private owners. The majority decided, however, that the act did not apply in cases where the government seized control. Under the ruling, union workers were forbidden to go out on strike while the federal government controlled the mines. Chief Justice Fred M. Vinson, who wrote the majority opinion, said the union's actions presented "a serious threat to orderly constitutional government and to the economic and social welfare of the nation."

The nation faced another crisis when the railroads and the unions could not agree on terms of a new contract. The remedies offered under the Railway Labor Act failed to resolve the dispute, and Truman set up yet another special board to hammer out an agreement. The railroads and most of the unions accepted the board's recommendation. But one union, representing trainmen and engineers, rejected the settlement and called for a strike. A frustrated Truman took control of the railroads. When the strike continued, the president put together a tough antistrike proposal and threatened to draft into the army all rail employees who did not return to work. Despite resolution of the matter, Truman pushed for legislation that would restrict strikes. The House passed the bill, but many viewed the proposal as extreme, and it did not get far in the Senate. Union supporters who had once praised Truman now condemned him as "the Number One strikebreaker."

CALL FOR ANTISTRIKE LAWS

Truman's emergency actions failed to reassure the public. Weary Americans witnessed a record number of strikes in the years following World War II. In 1946 alone, workers participated in almost five thousand strikes. As a result, businesses lost 116 million days of labor, triple the number of the previous year.

The strikes eroded public support for unions. People unconnected to the strikes lost jobs because factories had no coal to power their machinery or lacked raw material to make their products. The strikes alarmed people whose lives were directly affected by shortages of electricity, a discontinuation of rail service, and a lack of goods. They feared such widespread strikes put the nation's economy at risk.

National strikes against whole industries led to calls to prosecute unions under antitrust laws. Those who opposed unions claimed they acted as monopolies and should not be allowed to negotiate terms nationwide.

Other events contributed to the deteriorating reputation of unions among voters. As unions became more powerful, they began to compete against each other for members. In extreme cases, unions called strikes to protest job assignments or other inroads won by rival unions. These stop-work actions, called jurisdictional strikes, disrupted business and angered employers and customers alike. Unions also called for boycotts against companies not directly involved in labor disputes. For example, a union might organize a boycott of a retail store that carried dresses produced by a manufacturing plant embroiled in a battle over wages. In several cases, these secondary boycotts threatened to close down companies whose only connection to the labor dispute was as a customer of the manufacturer. Business groups complained that the Wagner Act controlled their activities, while unions had no similar restraints on their actions. They called on lawmakers to "equalize" the Wagner Act by putting the reins on what they viewed as out-of-control unions.

The high-profile cases of several union leaders charged with racketeering and extortion in the 1930s and 1940s led to further demands that Congress restrict union activities.

Responding to public pressure, several states passed anti-strike laws. In June 1946 Congress approved the Case bill, a restrictive piece of legislation that set up a federal board to mediate labor disputes, required a sixty-day cooling-off period before workers could go on strike, and banned boy-cotts and violent picketing. The bill allowed employers to sue unions for damages when they violated contracts. Truman considered the bill too drastic and vetoed it. Congress, by a slim five-vote margin, failed to override the veto, and the bill did not become law. The narrow victory, however, fore-shadowed future battles that labor might not be able to win.

Truman did, however, sign the Hobbs antiracketeering bill, which had originally been part of the Case bill. The bill aimed at preventing labor leaders from interfering with interstate commerce through robbery or extortion. In signing the bill, Truman reaffirmed his support of the Wagner Act and the rights guaranteed to unions. He said he had been assured that the bill was "not intended to deprive labor of any of its recognized rights, including the right to strike and to picket, and to take other legitimate and peaceful concerted action."

ANTIUNION POLITICIANS TAKE CONTROL

With public support for labor waning, antiunion activists saw an opening and took it. During the 1946 campaign for Congress and state legislatures, they supported Republican and conservative southern Democratic candidates who generally shared their views. Republicans swept the elections and took control of Congress with a majority over Democrats of 249 to 186 in the House and 51 to 44 in the Senate.

In the states, newly elected Republican lawmakers helped pass a number of laws that banned strikes or otherwise put restrictions on unions. By the end of 1947, spurred by an aggressive campaign led by the National Association of Manufacturers and the Chamber of Commerce, at least thirty states had passed laws to limit union activity. Only three retained laws that closely resembled the Wagner Act: New York, Rhode Island, and Connecticut. Several states prohibited boycotts and strikes; some also banned picketing, despite Supreme Court rulings that protected such activities under the Constitution's guarantee of free speech.

Union advocates in Congress had so far resisted the calls

to repeal or amend the Wagner Act. They feared any change would undermine unions and workers' rights. After the 1946 election, however, prounion supporters found themselves in the minority. In the eleven years since Congress had passed the Wagner Act, legislators had submitted 169 bills on the nation's labor policies. None had succeeded in altering the basic tenets of the original Wagner Act. With the seating of the eightieth Congress, however, that would change.

President Truman made it clear in his State of the Union message on January 6, 1947, that labor relations would be the nation's top priority. Americans watched his speech on television, the first live broadcast of a State of the Union address.

TRUMAN'S LABOR PLAN

In his speech, Truman reported the good news that Americans' standard of living had never been better, that production of goods and services was 50 percent higher than before the war, and that the nation's manufacturing sector continued to expand. But he expressed concern about rising prices and a continuation of what he termed the "economic warfare" during the previous year. Truman advised against "punitive" laws, but he called for a plan to ease relations between labor and management and reduce strikes and lockouts. "We must not, in order to punish a few labor leaders, pass vindictive laws which will restrict the proper rights of the rank and file of labor," he cautioned. Achieving smooth labor relations, Truman told Congress, depended upon management as well as labor. In 1946, he noted, strikes occurred because both management and labor failed to reach satisfactory agreements. "For that reason," the president said, "we must realize that industrial peace cannot be achieved merely by laws directed against labor unions."

Truman firmly supported a national labor policy based on "free collective bargaining" to determine wages and working conditions. In his labor proposals, the president outlined ways to improve the collective bargaining system and put an end to abuses by both labor and management.

Truman's four-point labor policy proposed an end to some union actions, such as strikes and boycotts used in disputes between unions; a fair minimum wage, national health care, and other federal benefits; mediation services through the Department of Labor to resolve labor disputes; and a commission to study ways to resolve labor issues.

In a second major policy statement, Truman urged Congress to limit the power of huge conglomerates that monopolized certain sectors of industry. "One of the gravest threats to our welfare," he said, "[is] the increasing concentration of power in the hands of a small number of giant organizations."

By 1947, fourteen million workers belonged to unions. Conservatives believed that the unions, not businesses, had grown too strong. This faction wanted laws that aided employers and restored the balance of power, which they believed currently favored unions.

FLURRY OF LABOR BILLS

During the first few weeks of January, legislators presented a flurry of bills in the Senate and the House on labor relations, several of which included the president's proposals. In all, the members proposed more than sixty labor bills during the first six months of the session. Most of the bills carried proposals that restricted union activity.

Response to the proposals was predictable. Labor leaders urged Congress to reject the restrictive bills, while business interests pushed for tough antiunion laws. The U.S. Chamber

President Harry S. Truman delivers his State of the Union address before a joint session of Congress on January 6, 1947. He called for a comprehensive labor law.

of Commerce and the National Association of Manufacturers called for immediate action and asked Congress to use antitrust laws to prevent unions from bargaining with entire industries. They also called for a ban on strikes among rival unions and on boycotts by those sympathetic to a union's cause. The groups urged businesses and unions to rely on voluntary arbitration to settle disputes.

Union leaders refused to work on any bill to amend the Wagner Act or to address union abuses. The CIO, AFL, and Railroad Brotherhoods all pledged to defeat legislation that restricted unions or limited collective bargaining. Proposals to ban closed and union shops particularly raised their ire. AFL president William Green told Congress that "loyal trade union members with a tradition of union-shop policy" would "refuse to work beside free riders and strikebreakers."

The fact that labor opposed a mandatory "cooling off" or waiting period before a strike gave the false impression that unions were "unreasoning groups of men who insist on rushing into strike action," a CIO spokesman said. He noted that unions and management had gone through lengthy negotiations before the strikes of a year ago.

The House Committee on Education and Labor opened its hearings on the labor issue in February 1947. Ten Democrats and fifteen Republicans served on the committee, including Richard M. Nixon of California and John F. Kennedy of Massachusetts, both future presidents. Nixon supported Hartley's bill; Kennedy opposed it.

For six weeks committee members heard testimony from more than 130 people. Nearly half (55) represented businesses. Another 27 spoke on labor's behalf. The committee also heard from public officials, other members of Congress, experts on labor issues, and members of the public. In addition, the committee waded through reports, analyses, letters, and other materials. In all, the official record of the hearings filled 3,873 pages. This became an issue later when critics charged that committee members had not taken enough time to digest the information before voting on the matter.

Members of Congress rely on committees to review bills, hold hearings, discuss the issues, make revisions, and present recommendations to the full House or Senate. During markup sessions committee members offer amendments, debate the merits of various proposals, and vote on a revised version of the bill. The bill then goes to the House or Senate for debate and final action. A committee's recommendation on a bill carries a good deal of weight once it is sent to the full Congress for consideration.

HARTLEY'S BILL

The Republican majority in the House focused its efforts on a rewrite of the Case bill, introduced by Representative Fred A. Hartley Jr., a Republican from New Jersey who chaired the House Committee on Education and Labor. Hartley presented his bill to the committee on April 10, without first holding committee discussions on the legislation or going through the customary markup sessions. The Democratic members of the committee charged that they had been excluded from the process of drawing up the bill and had had only a day for review before voting on it. Hartley said later that he had to prepare the bill "behind closed doors" because otherwise agents for the unions would have spread propaganda about its provisions and complicated the effort to get it passed.

On April 11, 1947, the House committee voted 18 to 6 in favor of the Hartley bill and referred it to the full House for debate. All fifteen Republican members of the committee voted for the bill. Three Democrats from southern states supported the measure, while one Democrat did not vote. Only six of the ten Democrats on the committee signed the minority report to Congress.

The sixty-six-page Hartley bill was a complex one that threatened to severely limit union activity. Although its sponsors called it a "labor bill of rights," Hartley's legislation included "the sharpest restrictions on labor unions ever attempted since collective bargaining became a powerful factor in American industrial life," the *New York Times* reported.

The bill sought to repeal much of the Wagner Act and included provisions to eliminate the National Labor Relations Board and replace it with a less powerful panel. The new board would have no power to enforce its decisions or to sue employers who refused to comply with the rulings. A separate system would mediate labor disputes, at the time the duty of the Labor Department. In addition, the bill would all but do away with closed shops, outlaw jurisdictional strikes and secondary boycotts, allow employers to sue unions for "triple damages" for "unlawful concerted activities" like sit-down strikes and jurisdictional work stoppages, and make unions subject to penalties under the antitrust laws.

The bill would also give the federal government power to seek court orders to stop strikes that threatened the public "health, safety or interest." It included a mandatory thirty-day waiting period and required a majority of workers to approve before a union could call a strike. Any member or sympathizer of the Communist Party would automatically be expelled from union membership.

The House turned down nine major amendments to the bill—all designed to make it more friendly to labor. The three amendments to win House approval added restrictions to the bill, including a ban on industry-wide bargaining.

Eager to pass a labor law quickly, House members limited debate on the bill to six hours. Less than a week after the bill left committee, the measure came to a vote. On April 17, 1947, amid cheers from supporters, the House approved the bill by a vote of 308 to 107—more than the 290 votes required to override a presidential veto. Ninety-three Democrats joined 215 Republicans in supporting the bill. The *New York Times* reported that the bill, if enacted, would "alter the whole range of labor policy built up in the Roosevelt era and reduce in every aspect the privileges of labor unions."

SENATE HEARINGS

While the House was considering the Hartley bill, the Senate reviewed its own labor legislation. The Senate Committee on

Labor and Public Welfare began five weeks of hearings on several labor bills on January 23. Lewis B. Schwellenbach, secretary of labor, began his testimony by opposing proposals to ban closed shops and bar unions from industry-wide negotiations. Schwellenbach also criticized a proposal in a labor bill proposed by Senators Robert Taft, Joseph H. Ball, and H. Alexander Smith that would set up a new federal mediation board to settle labor disputes, instead of relying on the Labor Department's conciliation service. Such a step would "impede industrial peace rather than further it," the labor secretary warned. When questioned about his support for closed union shops, Schwellenbach said the system allowed unions to bargain effectively with employers, which led to improvements in working conditions for all workers.

Leo Wolman, an economics professor and former adviser to a textile workers union, presented the opposite view. Unions, he told committee members, had become monopolies which would continue to disrupt the marketplace with demands. Wolman said that the steel or coal industry or the National Association of Manufacturers could not shut down operations as the unions had in 1946. "The Association [NAM] can talk but cannot press its will on its members," Wolman said. "The unions can force their will on their members." Wolman called on the senators to establish a system that would give employers and employees equal rights. He also supported the reestablishment of company unions, a ban on closed shops, and amendments to the Wagner Act that would give companies more power to oversee their labor force.

On March 7, John L. Lewis, the fiery head of the United Mine Workers, jousted with the members of the committee as he defended unions and spoke forcefully against amendments to the Wagner Act. Just twenty-four hours earlier, the

Labor leader John L. Lewis emphasizes his opposition to labor legislation during a dramatic appearance before the Senate Labor Committee on March 7, 1947.

Supreme Court had handed down its decision to uphold the conviction of Lewis and his union on contempt charges.

The appearance of the controversial union leader lent excitement to the proceedings. Big klieg lights lit the room as cameras recorded the performance on newsreels for later broadcast at movie theaters. News photographers crowded into the room to get a front-page shot of Lewis. The audience, packed into the hearing room, responded to the labor leader's words with occasional claps, laughter, and whispers.

The union leader spoke for an hour and a half, peering up from beneath bushy eyebrows to glare at questioners and reverting to his southern drawl to make a point and win chuckles from listeners. Unions, Lewis said, served an important role as the "inherent checks and balances in the economic system." Injunctions and government takeovers of industry, he noted, stymied the collective bargaining process and made it more difficult to settle labor disputes. "The operators need not ask for a change so long as they have the services of the Government to compel the men to work six days a week nine hours a day at present wages," Lewis said.

When asked what Congress could do to ensure that Americans had access to coal, he suggested that the government focus on "fair treatment of miners." He opposed any law that forced unions to give up their right to strike or engage in collective bargaining. "The question is whether you want to trade liberty for security," Lewis said. "If you want a totalitarian form of government, you can do all those things [avoid strikes and fights between labor and management]."

Lewis's testimony clashed with that given earlier in the morning by William L. McGrath, president of the Williamson Heater Company, an Ohio firm. McGrath characterized unions as "giant labor trusts and monopolies" that held the nation in their grip, and charged that the Wagner Act had "created a Frankenstein." Collective bargaining should be conducted only by local unions, not national groups, and unions should have to register with the federal government, McGrath said.

In other testimony that month, Paul M. Herzog, chairman of the National Labor Relations Board, told the committee that the nation would face "most unhappy consequences" if a new law impeded the collective bargaining system. The Wagner Act was "sound," Herzog said. He warned against eliminating any of the workers' rights guaranteed in the act.

During the committee hearings, several speakers charged that unions had been influenced, and in some cases taken over, by Communists. While it was true that Communist labor leaders had played a substantial role in the development of unions and continued to be involved on the local level, the American labor movement had made a strong shift to the right since the early days. At the national AFL convention in 1940, delegates had supported a resolution to ban the Communist Party in the United States. The United Mine Workers, under Lewis, barred Communists from union membership in 1929. When Lewis formed the CIO, however, he accepted support from the Communist labor movement. During the 1930s Communists strongly influenced the CIO, controlling about sixteen unions. That changed with the end of World War II and the rise of the Soviet Union's bid for international power. In the fall of 1946 delegates to the national CIO convention proclaimed that they "resent and reject efforts of the Communist Party or other political parties and their adherents to interfere in the affairs of the CIO."

TAFT'S BILL

After weeks of hearings, committee chairman Taft presented a sixty-two-page bill in April that reduced the power of national unions to negotiate with industries and put restrictions on union shops, strikes, and other union activities. It also allowed employers to try to persuade workers not to join unions as long as their statements contained "no threat of reprisal or force." The bill, one senator said, "contains everything, including the kitchen stove."

On April 11 the Senate Labor and Public Welfare Committee overruled its chairman, Senator Taft, and voted for a far less restrictive labor bill. The committee's Democrats and liberal Republicans joined forces to add three amendments to Taft's original bill. These amendments made it easier to set up union shops, barred employers from offering benefits or issuing threats to persuade workers not to join unions, and allowed all workers to join unions, except supervisors, who had the power to hire and fire other employees.

Senator Irving Ives, a Republican from New York, led the bipartisan coalition pushing for the more labor-friendly bill. During the next week, committee members negotiated and reworked the bill to attract more support. If Democrats as well as Republicans endorsed the bill, it had a better chance of being signed into law by President Truman.

New provisions added to the bill altered the makeup of the National Labor Relations Board, set up an independent mediation agency, prohibited employees as well as employers from unfair labor practices, and gave the NLRB and the attorney general authority to go to court to stop strikes in certain situations. Senator Wayne L. Morse, a Republican from Oregon, said the compromise the committee eventually reached was "one of the most remarkable legislative accomplishments on a committee level in the Congress in recent years."

On April 17, the same day the House approved the Hartley bill, the Senate Labor and Public Welfare Committee passed the revamped Taft bill by a vote of 11 to 2. As predicted, the changes persuaded all but two of the committee's more liberal members to support the bill. Only Claude Pepper of Florida and James E. Murray of Montana, both Democrats, voted against it. Although less restrictive than the House version, the Senate's bill promised a major overhaul of the Wagner Act. In presenting the bill to the full Senate, Taft said he might still propose amendments to toughen union restrictions.

RALLYING SUPPORT

Union advocates opposed both the Senate and the House versions of the labor bill. CIO delegates from across the nation visited members of Congress in April in a big push to persuade them to vote against any revision of the Wagner

Act. The rally did little to help their cause. With few supporters in Congress, union leaders turned to President Truman
to block any bill that they viewed as oppressive to labor.
Although Truman was not considered as strongly prounion
as Roosevelt, most political experts predicted he would need
the labor vote to win the presidential election in 1948.

The unions also looked for ways to improve their standing with the public and to consolidate their power. In March
the AFL set up a three-man panel to develop ways to settle
disputes between unions and prevent jurisdictional strikes.
CIO president Philip Murray, alarmed at the prospect of a law
that would severely curtail unions, proposed that the CIO
and AFL join together to fight antiunion forces. Representatives from the two union organizations met in May to discuss
a merger, but AFL leaders rejected the idea. The AFL, believ-
ing that the CIO had alienated Congress, chose to run its own
campaign against antiunion bills. Nevertheless, the meeting
served as a first step in the groups' eventual merger.

During the first three months of 1947, strikes decreased
dramatically. Work stoppages as the result of labor disputes
amounted to less than 10 percent of those recorded in the
first quarter of the previous year. With Congress considering tough new restrictions on unions, labor negotiators
worked hard to avoid actions that might turn public sentiment against them. The steelworkers' union and U.S. Steel
Corporation extended negotiations for several weeks after
the union contract expired in February. Electrical workers
approved contracts with Westinghouse and General Motors
in April without a strike.

However, labor disputes in two arenas, coal and telephone
service, captured the public's attention. Federal control of
the mines was due to expire on June 30, 1947, and Lewis's

threat of a renewed UMW strike hung over the nation during the hearings on the Taft-Hartley Act. Contract negotiations between the American Telephone and Telegraph Company, which controlled most of the nation's telephone lines, and the unions broke down in February 1947. In April the union's 330,000 telephone workers went out on strike, cutting off service to a third of the nation's telephones.

On April 22 AFL officers allocated $1.5 million for an "educational and publicity" drive to fight the pending labor legislation. The advertising campaign aimed to rally public support and persuade Americans to put pressure on President Truman to veto the bill and senators to sustain the veto. Union leaders conceded that support for the bill in the House was too overwhelming to fight off passage there. The telephone strike, however, lent credence to the argument that something had to be done to control big unions. The unions' refusal to work on amendments to the Wagner Act did not help their cause. Even with $1.5 million to spend, the AFL's ad campaign turned out to be too little too late.

SENATE DEBATES TAFT BILL

During the Senate debate on the Taft bill, conservative senators tried to push through an amendment to restrict industry-wide bargaining. The proposal barred national union organizations, like the UAW or the UMW, from negotiating for local unions unless the local organizations requested them to do so. Senator Taft led the effort to pass the measure, while Ives and Morse spoke forcefully against it. Taft argued that the large unions held "excessive power" to dictate contract terms and order actions by hundreds of local unions. He contended that local unions should be able to determine their own course. "This amendment will destroy no union,"

Taft declared. "It will take away the arbitrary power which national labor leaders have used against their own."

But Ives charged that labor opponents were merely using the argument of local control to defeat unions. In reality, the measure would weaken unions and put them at a disadvantage when bargaining with employers, he said. "This amendment," Ives asserted, "could tear trade unionism apart." The Republican defended the importance of unions to the economy, which, he said, might well come under "sinister influences" without unions. "The elimination of trade unionism as an influence in our society," he declared, "would probably contribute more than anything else to the destruction of freedom in America." In the end the proposal failed by one vote, 43 to 44.

On May 13, the Senate voted 68 to 24 to pass the Taft bill. The surprisingly large margin was enough to override a possible veto by President Truman. Democrats split their vote, with half in favor and half against the measure. Only three Republicans, including Senator Morse, opposed the Taft bill. Senator Alben W. Barkley, Democrat from Kentucky, led the opposition. He told his colleagues in the Senate that the bill was both "punitive" and "lacking in wisdom." Taft responded, "The whole effort here has been to restore equality between employer and employe, and to correct injustices arising out of laws passed by this Congress."

A COMPROMISE BILL

When the House and Senate approve separate bills on the same issue, the two bodies hold a joint conference to iron out the differences before sending a final bill to the president for signature. Usually the bills' authors participate in the conference along with an equal number of members from the

House and Senate. The conference members review the two bills and work out terms acceptable to the conference delegates. The compromise bill is then presented to the House and Senate for a vote. If both houses approve the conference recommendations, the bill is sent to the president to sign or veto. If the conference members cannot reach a consensus or if the House or the Senate does not approve the changes, neither bill becomes law. In that case, members of Congress can resubmit the bills during the next session, submit a new bill on the issue, or abandon the effort altogether.

The Hartley bill passed by the House and the Senate's more moderate Taft bill had several main differences: industry-wide bargaining by national unions (allowed by the Taft bill, banned by the Hartley bill), court orders to stop boycotts and jurisdictional strikes (allowed by Hartley, not by Taft), damages for companies (triple damages under Hartley), union shops (severe restrictions under Hartley, not under Taft), union regulation (rules on union operations under Hartley, none under Taft), the National Labor Relations Board (a new board with the sole duty of settling labor disputes under Hartley, an expanded board from three members to seven under Taft), and strikes (Hartley banned all strikes unless a majority of workers approved them beforehand, Taft put limits only on strikes that threatened the public interest).

The House bill also made it illegal for federal employees to strike, barred unions from contributing to national political campaigns, included a laundry list of unlawful activities by unions, applied the antitrust laws to unions, and banned mass picketing.

Both versions of the bill outlawed closed union shops, required union officials to take a loyalty oath declaring they were not Communists, guaranteed employers the right to speak about unions under the Constitution's free speech clause, barred unions from "unfair practices," and allowed the federal government to seek court injunctions for an eighty-day mediation period for strikes that threatened the public interest. They both set up a separate agency to mediate labor disputes.

The ten conference delegates spent the next week locked in debate over the two bills. A breakthrough occurred when the House members agreed to a Senate proposal to keep the NLRB and increase its members to five. Senators yielded to House delegates and went along with a provision that barred unions from contributing members' dues to political campaigns. Although the compromise measure permitted union shops, they could be set up only with the approval of a majority of all workers, not just of those voting. The new bill also allowed states to override the requirement that all workers join the union at workplaces with a union shop.

On May 28 the conference presented a compromise Taft-Hartley bill to Congress. The House was the first to consider the bill. Representative Hartley, who approved the revision of his harsher bill, declared that the compromise legislation was "fair to workers . . . fair to management—and above all it protects the interests of the general public." Hostility and bitterness marked the debate at times. Representative Mary T. Norton, a Democrat from New Jersey who opposed the bill, declared that "the labor baiters and the labor haters at long last are having a field day." Supporters of the bill greeted her comments with loud boos. Other Democrats joined the strong majority urging its passage. On June 4 House members voted 320 to 79 to pass the legislation.

Senator Taft opened the Senate's debate on the compromise bill the next day. The New Deal Democrats still in the

Senate bitterly denounced the measure, but they were in the minority even among members of their own party. Senator Murray mourned the "littered wreckage" of the Wagner Act, which he described as "the memorial to a gallant effort to bring democracy to our working people." Another New Deal senator, Claude Pepper, accused Congress of discriminating against the poor by supporting the bill.

Senator Ives said that measures needed to be taken to correct abuses and eliminate inequities in the existing labor laws. "No one could have listened to the hearings without knowing that something was wrong," he said. He blamed the labor unions for refusing to work on any legislation to address such concerns. "We received no help whatever from the representatives of organized labor," he said. Ives denied that the revised Taft-Hartley bill would "destroy" trade unions, as labor representatives asserted. "This legislation goes down the middle of the road," Ives insisted.

On June 6, after a long day of rancorous debate, the Senate voted for the Taft-Hartley bill 54 to 17. The large nonpartisan margin indicated that even a presidential veto probably would not stop the bill from becoming law. It also signified the end of an era when labor could automatically count on support from Congress and the Democratic Party.

The final version of the bill had the following provisions:

> • **Court remedies**. Allowed prosecution of unions that participated in strikes in violation of a contract, secondary boycotts and picketing, wildcat strikes, sympathy strikes, jurisdictional strikes, and other "unlawful concerted activities." It also allowed companies to seek damages from unions for jurisdictional strikes and boycotts.

- **Closed shops**. Prohibited closed shops.
- **Union shops**. Allowed union shops if a majority of all eligible workers voted for them. States had the right to bar union shops in their territory.
- **Banned union activities**. Banned secondary boycotts, jurisdictional strikes, and strikes conducted in violation of a union's contract. Made it illegal for workers to refuse to cross picket lines unless the labor dispute involved them directly.
- **Loyalty oaths**. Union officials (but not company officers) were required to take loyalty oaths to the United States, pledging that they were not Communists. Unions whose leaders did not take the oaths would be denied rights under the law.
- **National Labor Relations Board**. Expanded the board from three members to five and empowered the NLRB general counsel to seek injunctions against unions and management for violations of the act. Under the law, the NLRB was required to seek court injunctions to stop secondary boycotts.
- **Strikes**. Required a sixty-day notice before unions could go on strike over a new contract. Also gave the president power to seek a court injunction to stop any strike he considered a danger to the nation's health or safety. If the injunction were granted, union members could not strike for the next eighty days, during which labor and management would be required to work on a settlement.
- **Employers' speech**. Allowed employers to tell employees of their opposition to unions as long as they did not coerce or offer benefits to win their support against unions.

- **Supervisors**. Removed supervisors' unions from the law's protections.
- **Political activities**. Outlawed political contributions by unions and companies. Both could and did set up independent political action committees (PACs) to collect money for political causes.

A VETO AND AN OVERRIDE

With Congress's approval of the Taft-Hartley bill, pressure increased on the president to veto the bill. Thousands of union supporters at rallies in cities throughout the nation demanded that Truman reject the legislation. In New York City alone, sixty thousand or more CIO members marched up Eighth Avenue to Madison Square Garden wearing armbands and carrying banners that opposed the "Taft slave labor bill." CIO president Philip Murray told the crowd that the bill was "dangerously provocative," and New York City Mayor William O'Dwyer said that if enacted the act would bring wage cuts and another depression. Democratic leaders warned Truman that Republicans would win the presidency and Congress in 1948 if he did not support the unions' position.

On June 20, President Truman told Americans in a radio address that he was vetoing the Taft-Hartley bill. He portrayed the legislation as "bad for labor, bad for management, and bad for the country." In a sharply worded speech, the president called the bill "a shocking piece of legislation" that was "unfair to the working people of this country." He continued, "Unions exist so that laboring men can bargain with their employers on a basis of equality. Because of unions, the living standards of our working people have increased steadily until they are today the highest in the world."

Instead of being the "mild" measure that its supporters

claimed, Truman said the bill weakened unions, set back the nation's policy of collective bargaining, and harmed "every working man in the country." Far from encouraging labor and management to work together, Truman said, the legislation divided the two groups, sowed the "seeds of discord," and threatened the goal of constructing a better America. "It is filled with hidden legal traps that would take labor relations out of the plant, where they belong, and place them in the courts. . . . For the sake of the future of this Nation," the president concluded, "I hope that this bill will not become law."

Truman sent a note notifying Congress of his veto. Members of the House booed as Speaker Joseph W. Martin Jr. finished reading the president's message. Three minutes later, at 12:52 p.m., the House began its vote on the legislation. Loud cheers broke out as Martin announced the results, 331 to 83 to override Truman's veto, fifty-five votes more than needed. In the Senate, Taft and his allies pushed for equally quick action, but the bill's opponents began a filibuster— a technique that allows senators to talk nonstop to block action on bills they oppose.

After talking through the night and late into the next day, the small band of opponents finally abandoned their efforts and agreed to vote on the bill the following Monday. Truman sent a final message on June 23, claiming that the bill would "do serious harm to our country." From his hospital bed, the ailing Senator Robert Wagner, whose act had set the course of labor relations since 1935, also issued a statement urging his fellow lawmakers to sustain Truman's veto. The bill, Wagner declared, would destroy the work he had "so long labored to develop—industrial peace through democracy."

During three hours of debate, Senator Walter F. George, a Democrat from Georgia, said that he would vote against his

Secretary of the Senate Carl Loeffler (*center*) certifies Senate passage of the Taft-Hartley bill over President Harry S. Truman's veto on June 23, 1947. The bill's sponsors, Representative Fred Hartley (*left*) and Senator Robert Taft, look on.

party's leader because he believed the bill was the only way "to break the stranglehold of the labor bosses." He joined nineteen other Democrats, most from the South, in supporting the bill. Taft, the final speaker before the vote, said the bill would "swing the balance back to where the two sides [labor and management] can deal equally with each other."

Many members of the House stood on the sidelines watching the proceedings. Hundreds waited silently in the gallery as one by one the senators cast their votes. The final vote, 68 to 25, produced six more votes than needed to override Truman's veto. At 3:17 p.m. the Taft-Hartley Act—officially known as the Labor Management Relations Act—became the law of the land.

CHAPTER SIX

Labor Under the Taft-Hartley Act

The passage of the Taft-Hartley Act signaled a major shift in the nation's labor policies. The Wagner Act, by protecting the right of unions to bargain for workers, had put its faith in collective bargaining as the best way to resolve labor disputes. Under the 1935 law, labor relations had been largely in the hands of labor and management. The 1947 law, while it retained most of Wagner's collective bargaining provisions, gave much more power to state and federal governments to intervene in labor relations. Under Taft-Hartley, the federal government could demand cooling-off periods, federal courts could issue back-to-work orders, and states could bar union shops. In addition, the law returned some powers to employers and took away others from unions.

While much less restrictive toward unions than the original bill proposed by the House, the law nevertheless dismantled many of the labor-friendly protections of the Wagner Act. The new law made drastic changes in the operations of unions and the settlement of labor disputes. It barred unions from making direct contributions to prolabor politicians and required extensive records from unions filing complaints. It also allowed unions to be sued over jurisdictional strikes or other unfair practices. This exposed unions to hundreds of thousands of dollars in damages.

Perhaps the provision unions viewed as the most damaging was Section 14(b), which gave states the power to outlaw union shops' requirement that all workers join the union. Approximately two million workers belonged to union shops in 1947, when Congress passed the Taft-Hartley Act. Under Taft-Hartley, workers could set up union shops if a majority voted to do so. The law allowed unions to include a "security clause" that required all workers covered by a contract to pay union dues or lose their job. This gave the unions financial stability and ensured that those who benefited from collective bargaining paid their fair share of the union's expenses.

However, Section 14(b) allowed states to adopt "right-to-work" laws. Under such laws, workers could not be forced to join unions or pay union dues, but they nevertheless benefited from contracts negotiated by the union. As of 2009, twenty-two states had adopted right-to-work laws that, in effect, prohibited union shops within their borders.

The Taft-Hartley Act shut down the closed shops which accounted for almost 30 percent of union membership, about 4.2 million employees. It also nullified unions representing an estimated 100,000 foremen. In the past business owners had been required to bargain with these unions on the same basis as any other union. The new law did not cover these employees, who were classified as supervisors. Businesses could recognize their unions if they wished, but they no longer were required to bargain with them.

CALLS FOR REPEAL

Opponents immediately challenged the new law. The date Congress overrode Truman's veto, June 22, 1947, became known as "Labor's Black Monday." Within hours of the law's enactment, 18,000 UMW members walked off the job in coal mines in Pennsylvania, Alabama, West Virginia, and Ohio. Other unions threatened to test the new law's ban on strikes by participating in work stoppages of their own. AFL president William Green said the new law would result in "chaotic conditions" and "endanger our national economy." He announced a nationwide campaign to persuade Congress to repeal it. Unions nationwide charged that the law violated the U.S. Constitution and threatened to challenge it in court.

John L. Lewis, speaking at the AFL convention that summer, characterized the Taft-Hartley Act as "the first ugly, savage thrust of fascism in America." He charged that the law had been enacted "through an alliance between industrialists and the Republican majority in Congress, aided and abetted by those Democratic legislators who still believe in the institution of human slavery." When the AFL refused to go along with Lewis's demand to fight the anti-Communist pledge required of union officials, the fiery labor leader stormed out of the meeting. Other AFL members chose not to fight on Lewis's terms, but they, too, opposed the law. The U.S. Supreme Court overturned the required loyalty oath in 1965, but most other challenges to the law failed.

Workers repeatedly voted to be represented by unions in elections run by the NLRB, as required under the Taft-Hartley Act. Unions garnered support from an average of 87 percent of workers voting in the NLRB elections. In August 1947, less than two months after the bill became law, polls revealed that 54 percent of those familiar with the law disapproved of it. Earlier polls, however, indicated that a majority of Americans also had disliked the Wagner Act.

The passage of the act had an effect on both political parties in the 1948 national elections the following November. Many Republicans thought the passage of the Taft-Hartley Act would benefit them at the polls, but they turned out to be wrong. Facing a tough election, Democratic candidates, headed by President Harry S. Truman, called for an outright repeal of the act. Even though Democrats had helped pass the law, labor voters supported Truman and his party on election day. Democrats regained control of both houses of Congress, while Republicans lost seventy-five seats in the House and eight seats in the Senate. Perhaps more than anything else, the passage of the Taft-Hartley Act spurred the unions to become involved in politics on the state and federal level. Labor's well-organized grassroots campaign to "turn out our enemies who passed the Taft-Hartley Act" helped secure the Democrats' victory.

Less than a week after the election, the Truman administration began discussions on repealing the law and replacing it with a less restrictive one. On November 15 Maurice J. Tobin, Truman's secretary of labor, predicted that Congress would repeal the act within thirty days. But by the end of December, administration staffers still had not agreed on when to launch the repeal effort in Congress or what to present in its place. Labor leaders pushed for an immediate repeal of the act, arguing that the longer the repeal effort was delayed, the less likely it would pass. Others, however, feared that conservatives in Congress might block a repeal if no other legislation was proposed to replace it.

In January 1949 President Truman presented his plan to repeal the act. His proposal reinstated most of the provisions of the old Wagner Act, but retained the Taft-Hartley ban on labor abuses such as "unjustifiable" jurisdictional strikes and boycotts. Instead of Taft-Hartley's court injunction and eighty-day cooling-off period in national emergency cases, Truman's bill gave the president power to call strikers back to work. It also set up a board that would propose settlements to such disputes within twenty-five days. Acceptance of the board's recommendations by labor and management would be voluntary.

Congress heard a replay of the pros and cons of the Taft-Hartley bill during hearings held that spring. By June it became obvious that conservative Republicans along with southern Democrats would block any attempt to ease union regulations. Labor balked at Senator Taft's amendment, which would allow injunctions and plant takeovers by the federal government. In the end, labor rejected the new bill altogether after the Senate approved Taft's amendment and other limits on union activities. The bill died in Congress, as did all future efforts to repeal the Taft-Hartley Act.

The failure to repeal the Taft-Hartley Act underscored for labor leaders the importance of unifying their efforts. After existing as rivals for two decades, the American Federation of Labor and the Congress of Industrial Organizations merged into one national labor group, the AFL-CIO, in 1955. George Meany, who led the AFL after the death of William Green in 1952, became the new organization's first president.

PRESIDENTIAL INJUNCTIONS

Despite his opposition to the Taft-Hartley Act, Truman invoked the law ten times to stop strikes that he said endangered the nation. Not all required an injunction; some were settled during the fact-finding phase. In the spring of 1948

George Meany (*left*) and Walter Reuther (*right*) symbolically share control of a king-size gavel as they announce the merger of the American Federation of Labor and the Congress of Industrial Organizations in New York City in December 1955.

Truman relied on the act to halt a strike by coal miners. UMW leader John L. Lewis told miners they could decide for themselves whether to continue the strike. Most of the miners chose not to return to the mines. A federal judge found Lewis and other UMW officers guilty of contempt but took no other action because most of the miners had returned to work by then.

In May 1948 Truman again relied on the Taft-Hartley Act in a dispute between American Telephone and Telegraph Company and the workers' union. This time the union supported Truman's action, while the company criticized it. Workers wanted the board of inquiry to conduct a review of their request for a wage increase.

Truman invoked the act to halt coal strikes a second time in 1950. Again, miners continued their strike in defiance of government. Wildcat strikes—work stoppages not sanctioned by the union—continued to cripple the industry. The attorney general sued, asking that the union be found in contempt of court. The miners were still on strike when a federal judge ruled that the government had failed to prove its case.

The court decision in the coal strike and the actions of the miners raised questions about the effectiveness of the Taft-Hartley Act. Both proponents and opponents of the law agreed that the provision allowing injunctions in a national emergency "had gone awry" if an "aggressive labor leader" like Lewis could "march a horse and wagon right through it." Proponents of the law called for amendments to tighten its restrictions. They favored a complete ban on industry-wide bargaining. Opponents called for a return to the Wagner Act, which had no provision for back-to-work court orders. Congress made several attempts to revise the law, but none of the proposals won enough support to pass.

In 1959 President Dwight D. Eisenhower also used the law to settle labor disputes. A conflict arose between the United Steelworkers union and the steel companies involving the union's demand for wage increases and the firms' attempt to change work rules. The companies wanted to be able to replace workers with machinery more easily. Neither side was willing to back down on the issues.

As the strike dragged on, steel supplies ran short. The economy, which relied heavily on steel for many products, began to feel the effects of the strike. On October 9, with no resolution in sight, Eisenhower asked the court to order a halt to the strike. The union challenged the court's back-to-work order, and on November 7 the Supreme Court, by an 8 to 1 vote, upheld the emergency injunction. In its decision, the Court affirmed the constitutionality of Taft-Hartley injunctions.

"The statute does recognize [the public's] rights . . . to have unimpeded . . . production in industries vital to the national health or safety," the Court ruled.

Union members resumed work after a 116-day strike—the longest steel strike in the nation's history. Union leaders, however, asserted they would not accept the companies' new work rules and would continue the strike after the eighty-day waiting period ended. Settlement came before that, however, on January 5, 1960, when the steel producers agreed to a generous wage and benefit package and no change in work rules. Steel officials claimed that the union held "vastly" more power than they did.

LANDRUM-GRIFFIN ACT AND LABOR REFORM

In 1957 a special committee chaired by Senator John L. McClellan, an Arkansas Democrat, investigated charges of corruption in the nation's labor unions. The McClellan Committee focused on the International Brotherhood of Teamsters, the largest union in the country, and its president, Dave Beck. After weeks of hearings, the Senate committee uncovered links between the Teamsters and organized crime. It also found evidence of other illegal activities, including racketeering and misuse of union funds. As a result of the investigation, federal prosecutors won the convictions of Beck and several other labor leaders. The AFL-CIO expelled the Teamsters from its membership, and James Hoffa, who faced charges of his own but was acquitted, took control of the union.

The disclosure of corruption and illegal activities tarnished the image of labor unions among the American people and Congress. An outcry arose for new laws to oversee union activities. In response, Congress passed the Labor-

Management Reporting and Disclosure Act in 1957, which added more union restrictions to the Taft-Hartley Act. The law, jointly proposed by Representative Phillip M. Landrum of Georgia and Senator Robert P. Griffin of Michigan, put the federal government in charge of overseeing union activities. Under the act, also known as the Landrum-Griffin Act, unions had to submit yearly reports on their finances to the Labor Department and make financial records available to members. The law also barred anyone with a criminal record from holding office in a union. Title I of the law set up rules to protect workers from being harassed or coerced by union bosses. It guaranteed free elections, secret ballots for votes on increases in dues, and fair hearings for members disciplined by their unions.

In 1962 President John F. Kennedy issued an executive order that allowed federal employees to unionize for the first time. The Federal Service Labor-Management Relations Act, passed by Congress in 1978, formally established the right of federal employees to form and join unions. The act, administered by the Federal Labor Relations Authority, bans federal workers from participating in strikes, slowdowns, work stoppages, and picketing that interferes with governmental operations.

Union supporters made another attempt to repeal Section 14(b) of the Taft-Hartley Act in 1965. They had tried unsuccessfully to ban right-to-work laws in the states for years. Now that Democrats controlled Congress and President Lyndon B. Johnson was winning support for his Great Society reform programs, the timing seemed right for a new labor bill. Johnson, as a representative from Texas, had voted to override Truman's veto when the original Taft-Hartley Act passed. But as president he pledged to back the bill to ban right-to-work laws in exchange for labor's support in the 1964 presidential election. The bill passed the House of Representatives on a vote of 221 to 203, but it ran into trouble in the Senate when a coalition of Republicans and southern Democrats opposed it. Minority Leader Everett Dirksen, a staunch supporter of the right-to-work laws, led a filibuster and blocked the Senate bill. A majority of senators backed the measure, but its supporters did not have the sixty-seven votes required at that time to break the filibuster. (The rules were later changed to reduce the required votes to sixty.) No other serious effort to overturn right-to-work laws has been introduced in Congress since then.

In the mid–1970s, labor leaders in the construction business launched another attempt to amend the Taft-Hartley Act. This time they took aim at the ban on secondary boycotts. Under the 1947 law, workers in the building trade who had a grievance with a subcontractor could not legally picket the company at a construction site where other firms also worked. Both houses of Congress passed a bill in 1975 that would have lifted the ban, but President Gerald Ford vetoed it. In his message to Congress on the veto, Ford said he believed the bill would lead to "greater, not lesser, conflict in the construction industry." The secretary of labor, who had supported the bill, resigned to protest Ford's action. The bill died when Congress failed to muster enough votes to override the president's veto.

Union supporters undertook yet another effort to reform the labor law in 1977 and 1978 after Democrats regained control of Congress and the White House. They resubmitted the construction bill, but a coalition of Republicans and southern Democrats defeated it in the House. A second bill, calling for reforms in the union election process, won initial support in the House, but a coalition of Republicans and southern Democrats in the Senate blocked the bill. Supporters tried and failed six times to end a filibuster on the measure. The bill eventually died.

While union advocates could not win support for reforms in the labor law, they did manage to fight off amendments designed to further weaken unions. In 1996 President Bill Clinton, a Democrat, vetoed the Teamwork for Employees and Managers Act, a Republican-sponsored amendment that would have lifted the Taft-Hartley Act's ban on company unions. The bill passed the House by a vote of 221 to 202 and the Senate by a vote of 53 to 46. Congress did not attempt to override the veto. In his veto message, Clinton declared that the bill would "undermine the system of collective bargaining" and "abolish protections that ensure independent and democratic representation in the workplace."

LABOR RELATIONS TODAY

When the Taft-Hartley Act became law in 1947, a large majority of Americans approved of unions. In 2009 fewer than half said they considered labor unions to be beneficial. While 66 percent of those polled agreed that unions helped their own members, 51 percent said that unions hurt the U.S. economy, according to a Gallup poll. The results reflected Americans' frustration over the economic downturn that brought down big corporations and seriously impacted the stock market. In the eyes of many, labor shared some of the blame for the excesses that led to the crisis.

Likewise, union membership has declined. In 1947 unions represented 32 percent of workers in private companies. In 2009 only 7.2 percent of nongovernmental workers and 12.4 percent overall belonged to unions. Since the passage of the Taft-Hartley Act in 1947, the American workplace and its employees have undergone notable changes that have had a negative impact on union membership. Many large companies, which once employed heavily unionized blue-collar workers, have moved their manufacturing operations overseas. In today's workforce, a higher concentration of employees hold clerical and white-collar jobs, which have not traditionally been represented by unions. In addition, many firms now contract with overseas workers to perform service jobs such as telemarketing, technical assistance, and customer service. Other companies use more part-timers, who often do not qualify for union membership or its benefits, instead of hiring full-time employees.

Several other factors have played a role in the waning influence of unions: a number of firms have relocated to southern states, where right-to-work laws are in force; various unions compete for the same members; and unions have difficulty winning elections to organize at workplaces.

A 2001 Supreme Court case, *National Labor Relations Board v. Kentucky River Community Care Inc.*, also set back the union cause when it classified doctors and nurses as supervisors. In 2006 the NLRB issued its own ruling, which broadened the definition of supervisor to include workers who gave assignments to other employees and were held responsible for their work. Critics argued that only employees with the authority to hire and fire should qualify as supervisors. The NLRB decision could bar accountants, lawyers, and a number of other professionals from joining unions that qualify for protections under the law. Even with the new NLRB rules, the question of who qualifies as a supervisor under Taft-Hartley remains unclear. In 2007 a federal court reversed an NLRB decision that a registered nurse was a supervisor.

The Taft-Hartley Act has remained in force for more than sixty years. Despite labor's determined efforts to repeal or revise the act and attempts by employers to strengthen their position under the statute, the law retains most of the major provisions it had when Congress enacted it in 1947.

The number of strikes and lockouts has dipped steadily over the past three decades as union membership among private industry workers has declined. The Bureau of Labor Statistics shows that work stoppages involving 1,000 or more workers occurred 145 times in 1981, idling 729,000 workers for more than 16.9 million days' worth of work. The bureau logged forty similar work stoppages in 1991 and only fifteen in 2008.

Presidents have used the Taft-Hartley provision to end work stoppages thirty-six times. President Jimmy Carter invoked the law in 1978 to obtain a temporary injunction to force coal miners to go back to work. A federal judge turned down Carter's request, ruling that the government had not proved that the strike had created a national emergency.

Since then, no other president had sought an injunction under Taft-Hartley until George W. Bush used the law to order ten thousand West Coast port operators back to work in the fall of 2002. The marine companies involved in the dispute had locked employees out of their workplace after contract negotiations broke down. It was the first time ever that a president had used the law's injunction to end a lockout. The union and port operators agreed to a contract the following January that gave workers an increased pension and allowed firms to adopt new high-tech methods to handle cargo.

In the years since Taft-Hartley was enacted, the federal government has expanded its reach into labor-management affairs. Federal legislation has addressed many of the poor

Nurses rally in October 2006 in Los Angeles to protest a ruling by the National Labor Relations Board preventing nurse supervisors from belonging to a union.

conditions unions worked for years to correct. The Fair Labor Standards Act, originally passed in 1938 and amended many times since then, sets minimum wage and overtime pay standards as well as minimum age and child labor requirements. The Occupational Safety and Health Act (OSHA), passed in 1970, requires private businesses to meet health and safety standards set and administered by the federal OSHA program. A 1974 law, the Employee Retirement Income Security Act, requires private industry to follow certain rules if they choose to set up retirement and health insurance plans for employees. While the rules are mandatory, the plans are not. Employers do not have to offer such benefits to workers if they do not wish to. In 1993, Congress passed the Family and Medical Leave Act, which requires companies with fifty or more workers to hold an employee's job for up to twelve weeks while he or she takes time off because of illness or to care for ill family members or newborns.

A variety of federal laws regulate compensation programs for workers injured on the job. One in particular provides payments and medical benefits to coal miners disabled from black lung disease. Also in place are laws to protect "whistleblowers," employees who report violations of laws by their employers. The Equal Employment Opportunity Commission, set up in 1965 under the Civil Rights Act of 1964, oversees laws that make it illegal to discriminate against an employee at the workplace because of race, color, religion, sex, national origin, advancing age, disability, or genetic information. It is also illegal to discriminate against a worker because he or she complained about discriminatory behavior, filed a discrimination charge, or participated in an employment discrimination investigation or lawsuit.

EMPLOYEE FREE CHOICE ACT

The labor movement has abandoned its fight to repeal the Taft-Hartley Act, but it continues to push for legislation to make it easier to organize workers. Its latest effort is the campaign to pass the Employee Free Choice Act. The legislation would ease restrictions on organizing unions at the workplace. After the bill died in the face of a threatened filibuster by Republicans in the Senate in 2007, supporters reintroduced the measure to a more receptive Democratic Congress in 2010. Its prospects looked dim, however, after voters elected a Republican House in November 2010.

Critics have dubbed the legislation the "Card Check Bill" because it allows workers to establish a union if a majority signs cards requesting one. Under the present system, union organizers have to hold an election monitored by the NLRB after first collecting signed cards from at least 30 percent of the employees. The card-check process is quicker and simpler than holding elections and allows employers less time to campaign against the union, say proponents.

A study conducted by Cornell University professor Kate Bronfenbrenner found that a majority of employers had used scare tactics in persuading workers to vote against unions. The study, released in May 2009, reported that companies had fired union organizers and threatened to close plants, cut wages, and reduce benefits during organizing campaigns. The results were based on more than one thousand union elections held from 1999 through 2003. The U.S. Chamber of Commerce criticized the study as biased toward labor.

Most of the opposition to the bill has come from business interests, including the Chamber of Commerce. The measure, they assert, would deprive workers of their right to a secret ballot and would allow union organizers to coerce workers into supporting a union.

The bill would provide labor with its best chance to build membership in years, say supporters. Elizabeth Shuler, the secretary-treasurer of the AFL-CIO, said the bill would help reverse the decline in union membership that has occurred in the six decades since the Taft-Hartley Act became law.

A BETTER FUTURE FOR UNIONS?

Meanwhile, unions have begun to reach out to a much more diverse group of workers. A surge in membership in 2007 and 2008 indicates the strategy is paying off. Bureau of Labor records show that unions added 311,000 members in 2007 and 428,000 members in 2008, the largest increase in twenty-five years. By the end of 2008, more than 16 million workers belonged to unions. Most of the gain occurred among government workers, 36.8 percent of whom are union members.

When the Taft-Hartley Act became law, most union members were white males, and only a few of the jobs traditionally held by women had union coverage. Results from a study by the Center for Economic Policy Research (CEPR) released in 2008 show that women now make up 45 percent of union membership, and more minority workers are joining unions. "We've seen a big increase over the last quarter century of women in unions, particularly as the unionization of the service sector expands," said John Schmitt, the economist who authored the CEPR study. "The fastest growth in union membership is among Latinos, and there's a bigger share of African Americans in unions than in the workforce as a whole. There's a lot of change in the movement." AFL-CIO's Shuler said the trend is encouraging. "Unions have been pushing hard to open their doors," she said.

During the presidential election of 2008, unions produced 250,000 workers for the Obama campaign, and two-thirds of union members voted for the Democratic candidate. Such activism, say labor leaders, indicates an underlying energy among members that unions can tap to strengthen the labor movement. "If organized labor can turn out a quarter of a million workers to elect a president, why can't a similar force be mobilized to kick off a huge recruitment drive?" asks labor analyst Kim Moody. "The goal," he says, "would not be just a few thousand more bargaining units, but a movement aimed at changing the balance of social forces in America . . . even as it recruits new union members."

From Bill to Law

For a proposal to become a federal law, it must go through many steps:

In Congress:

1. A bill is proposed by a citizen, a legislator, the president, or another interested party. Most bills originate in the House and then are considered in the Senate.

2. A representative submits the bill to the House (the first reading). A senator submits it to the Senate. The person (or people) who introduces the bill is its main sponsor. Other lawmakers can become sponsors to show support for the bill. Each bill is read three times before the House or the Senate.

3. The bill is assigned a number and referred to the committee(s) and subcommittee(s) dealing with the topic. Each committee adopts its own rules, following guidelines of the House and the Senate. The committee chair controls scheduling for the bill.

4. The committees hold hearings if the bill is controversial or complex. Experts and members of the public may testify. Congress may compel witnesses to testify if they do not do so voluntarily.

5. The committee reviews the bill, discusses it, adds amendments, and makes other changes it deems necessary during markup sessions.

6. The committee votes on whether to support the bill, oppose it, or take no action on it and issues a report on its findings and recommendations.

7. A bill that receives a favorable committee report goes to the Rules Committee to be scheduled for consideration by the full House or Senate.

8. If the committee delays a bill or if the Rules Committee fails to schedule it, House members can sign a discharge motion and call for a vote on the matter. If a majority votes to release the bill from committee, it is scheduled on the calendar as any other bill would be. Senators may vote to discharge the bill from a committee as well. More commonly, though, a senator will add the bill as an amendment to an unrelated bill in order to get it past the committee blocking it. Or a senator can request that a bill be put directly on the Senate calendar, where it will be scheduled for debate. House and Senate members can also vote to suspend the rules and vote directly on a bill. Bills passed in this way must receive support from two thirds of those voting.

9. Members of both houses debate the bill. In the House, a chairperson moderates the discussion and each speaker's time is limited. Senators can speak on the issue for as long as they wish. Senators who want to block the bill may debate for hours in a tactic known as a filibuster. A three-fifths vote of the Senate is required to stop the filibuster (cloture), and talk on the bill is then limited to one hour per senator.

10. Following the debate, the bill is read section by section (the second reading). Members may propose amendments, which are voted on before the final bill comes up for a vote.

11. The full House and Senate then debate the entire bill and those amendments approved previously. Debate continues until a majority of members vote to "move the previous question" or approve a special resolution forcing a vote.

12. A full quorum—at least 218 members in the House, 51 in the Senate—must be present for a vote to be held. A member may request a formal count of members to ensure a quorum is on hand. Absent members are sought when there is no quorum.

13. Before final passage, opponents are given a last chance to propose amendments that alter the bill; the members vote on them.

14. A bill needs approval from a majority of those voting to pass. Members who do not want to take a stand on the issue may choose to abstain (not vote at all) or merely vote present.

15. If the House passes the bill, it goes on to the Senate. By that time, bills often have more than one hundred amendments attached to them. Occasionally, a Senate bill will go to the House.

16. If the bill passes in the same form in both the House and the Senate, it is sent to the clerk to be recorded.

17. If the Senate and the House version differ, the Senate sends the bill to the House with the request that members approve the changes.

18. If the two houses disagree on the changes, the bill may go to conference, where members appointed by the House and the Senate work out a compromise if possible.

19. The House and the Senate vote on the revised bill agreed to in conference. Further amendments may be added and the process repeated if the Senate and the House version of the bill differ.

20. The bill goes to the president for a signature.

To the President:

1. If the president signs the bill, it becomes law.

2. If the president vetoes the bill, it goes back to Congress, which can override his veto with a two-thirds vote in both houses.

3. If the president takes no action, the bill automatically becomes law after ten days if Congress is still in session.

4. If Congress adjourns and the president has taken no action on the bill within ten days, it does not become law. This is known as a pocket veto.

The time from introduction of the bill to the signing can range from several months to the entire two-year session. If a bill does not win approval during the session, it can be reintroduced in the next Congress, where it will have to go through the whole process again.

Notes

Chapter One

p. 16, "grievous Oppression . . .": Foster Rhea Dulles, *Labor in America: A History*, 3rd ed. New York: Thomas Y. Crowell Company, 1966, 15.

p. 20, "Critics contend . . .": Carl Smith, "The Dramas of Haymarket," Chicago: Chicago Historical Society and the Trustees of Northwestern University, 2000. www.chicagohs.org/dramas/

p. 21, "It is the duty . . .": Walter Gilberti, "The Haymarket Frame-up and the Origins of May Day," May 13, 2009, World Socialist website. www.wsws.org/articles/2009/may2009/hay3-m13.shtml

p. 22, "the most dangerous . . .": Linda Atkinson, *Mother Jones: The Most Dangerous Woman in America*. New York: Crown Publishers, Inc., 1978, 1.

p. 23, "My life work . . .": Atkinson, *Mother Jones*, 2.

p. 24, "By 1904 . . .": Gary M. Fink, "Labor Unions," AFL-CIO website, cited in George Ochoa and Melinda Cory, *Facts About the 20th Century*. New York: H. W. Wilson, 2001. www.hwwilson.com/print/20thcentury.pdf

Chapter Two

p. 26, "cost the railroads . . .": Keith Ladd, "The Pullman Strike: Chicago, 1894," Kansas Heritage Group, 1998. www.kansasheritage.org/pullman/index.html

p. 26, "compelling or inducing . . .": Ladd, "The Pullman Strike: Chicago, 1894."

p. 30, "a wholesale rounding up . . .": "Forty-Three More Indicted," *New York Times*, July 20, 1894. www.nytimes.com

p. 31, "The strong arm . . .": *In re Debs*, 158 U.S. 564 (1895).

p. 28, "Workers could not attend . . .": Linda Atkinson, *Mother Jones: The Most Dangerous Woman in America*. New York: Crown Publishers, Inc., 1978, 81, 82–84.

p. 28, "While the men . . .": "Digging for Survival: The Child Miners," International Labour Organization, 2005, 5.

pp. 28–29, "Company Mining Towns": Lawrence W. Boyd, "The Company Town," *EH.Net Encyclopedia*, ed. Robert Whaples, January 30, 2003. http://eh.net/encyclopedia/article/boyd.company.town

p. 29, "In 1913 the average . . .": Helen S. Stinson, compiler, "Index of Fatalities in West Virginia Coal Mines 1883–1925," from *The Reports of Mine Inspectors*, Allegheny Regional Family History Society, 1985. http://pages.swcp.com/~dhickman/wvcmf/wvcmf.html

p. 32, "the union was ordered . . .": *Loewe* v. *Lawlor*, 208 U.S. 274 (1908).

p. 36, "If you don't . . .": Pauline Newman. "Letters to Michel and Hugh from P.M. Newman," May 1951, Kheel Center for Labor-Management Documentation and Archives, Cornell University ILR School. www.ilr.cornell.edu/trianglefire/texts/

letters/newman_letter.html?location=Sweatshops+and+Strikes

pp. 36–37, "Working in the Children's Corner": "The Uprising of 20,000 and the Triangle Shirtwaist Fire," AFL-CIO website. www.aflcio.org/aboutus/history/history/uprising_fire.cfm

p. 39, "Out of that terrible . . .": Annelise Orleck, *Common Sense and a Little Fire: Women and Working-Class Politics in the United States, 1900–1965*. Chapel Hill: University of North Carolina Press, 1995, 130–131.

p. 40, "The rights and interests . . .": *Cleveland Citizen* (August 26, 1902), cited in Harry A. Millis and Emily Clark Brown, *From the Wagner Act to Taft-Hartley: A Study of National Labor Policy and Labor Relations*. Chicago: University of Chicago Press, 1950, 15, note 44.

p. 41, "conspiracy in restraint . . .": *United Mine Workers et al v. Red Jacket Consolidated Coal & Coke Co.*, 18 F. 2d 839 (C.C.A. 4, 1927), cited in Millis and Brown, *From the Wagner Act to Taft-Hartley*, 15, note 44.

p. 44, "without interference . . .": Millis and Brown, *From the Wagner Act to Taft-Hartley*, 19.

p. 45, "be free from . . .": 47 U.S. Stat. 70 (Norris–La Guardia Anti-Injunction Act), cited in Millis and Brown, *From the Wagner Act to Taft-Hartley*, 20–21.

Chapter Three

pp. 50–51, "Polls conducted . . .": Foster Rhea Dulles, *Labor in America: A History*, 3rd ed. New York: Thomas Y. Crowell Company, 1966, 276.

pp. 53–54, "Employees have as clear . . .": *National Labor Relations Board* v. *Jones and Laughlin Steel Corporation*, 301 U.S. 1 (1937).

p. 55, "private corporations . . .": Dulles, *Labor in America*, 277–278.

p. 57, "regulation which is reasonable . . .": *West Coast Hotel Company* v. *Parrish*, 300 U.S. 379 (1937).

p. 57, "interfere with . . .": *Mackay Radio* v. *NLRB*, 304 US 345–46 (1938).

pp. 57–58, "the same arbitrary . . .": *Hunt* v. *Crumboch*, 325 US 821 (1945).

p. 58, "must remain as . . .": Dulles, *Labor in America*, 287.

Chapter Four

p. 63, "armed with baseball . . .": Louis Stark, "Steel Plant Siege Is Begun by Union," *New York Times*, May 30, 1937, 1.

p. 63, "Get off the field . . .": William Bork, "Massacre at Republic Steel," Illinois Labor History Society. www.kentlaw.edu/ilhs/republic.htm

p. 66, "never recognize . . .": Mary Heaton Vorse, "Labor's New Millions," Internet Archive, www.archive.org/stream/laborsnewmillion00vorsrich/laborsnewmillion00vorsrich_djvu.txt

p. 68, "Over the same . . .": Harry A. Millis and Emily Clark Brown, *From the Wagner Act to Taft-Hartley: A Study of National Labor Policy and Labor Relations*. Chicago: University of Chicago Press, 1950, 80–85.

p. 68, "The board's activities . . .": Millis and Brown, *From the Wagner Act to Taft-Hartley*, 88–89.

p. 69, "The Wagner board . . .": Millis and Brown, *From the Wagner Act to Taft-Hartley*, 89.

p. 69, "By 1946 . . .": Millis and Brown, *From the Wagner Act to Taft-Hartley*, 93.

p. 69, "Labor has gained . . .": Foster Rhea Dulles, *Labor in America: A History*, 3rd ed. New York: Thomas Y. Crowell Company, 1966, 314.

p. 69, "Join the C.I.O. . . .": Vorse, "Labor's New Millions."

p. 71, "That year more than . . .": Dulles, *Labor in America*, 326–327.

p. 75, "Over the course . . .": Dulles, *Labor in America*, 343.

p. 76, "U.S. Army carried . . .": Dulles, *Labor in America*, 343–344.

p. 76, "vicious and continuous . . .": Dulles, *Labor in America*, 340–341.

Chapter Five

p. 79, "to cushion . . .": Foster Rhea Dulles, *Labor in America: A History*, 3rd ed. New York: Thomas Y. Crowell Company, 1966, 347.

p. 81, "Hundreds of smaller . . .": Harry A. Millis and Emily Clark Brown, *From the Wagner Act to Taft-Hartley: A Study of National Labor Policy and Labor Relations*. Chicago: University of Chicago Press, 1950, 312–313.

p. 81, "As the new year . . .": Dulles, *Labor in America*, 349.

pp. 81–82, "an evil, demoniac . . .": Dulles, *Labor in America*, 351.

p. 82, "a serious threat . . .": *United States* v. *United Mine Workers*, 330 U.S. 258 (1947).

p. 83, "the Number One . . .": Dulles, *Labor in America*, 352–353.

p. 83, "In 1946 alone, . . .": Jordan Ludwig, "The Passage and Events Surrounding the Taft-Hartley Act: An Analysis," *Janus*, Spring 2007, 1–2. www.janus.umd.edu/issues/sp07/Ludwig_Taft-HartleyAct.pdf

p. 85, "not intended to . . .": Walter H. Waggoner, "Hobbs Bill Is Law," *New York Times*, July 4, 1946, 1.

pp. 86–87, "In his speech . . .": Harry S. Truman, "State of the Union Address," January 6, 1947.

p. 87, "One of the gravest…": Harry S. Truman, "Letter to the Chairman of the House Judiciary Committee on the Problem of Concentration of Economic Power," July 9, 1949, www.trumanlibrary.org/publicpapers/index.php?pid=1166&st=&st1=103. "Hits Labor Study Plan; Chamber Says Need Is Prompt Legislation by Congress," *New York Times*, January 30, 1947, 14.

pp. 88–89, "Green told Congress . . . into strike action": Joseph A. Loftus, "CIO Asks Congress Go Slow on Laws," *New York Times*, January 10, 1947, 11.

p. 89, "For six weeks . . .": Millis and Brown, *From the Wagner Act to Taft-Hartley*, 366–367.

p. 90, "Hartley said later . . .": Millis and Brown, *From the Wagner Act to Taft-Hartley*, note, 369–370.

p. 90, "Although its sponsors . . .": William S. White, "Lower Chamber Votes Restrictions on Unions With Acclaim, *New York Times*, April 18, 1947, 1.

p. 91, "alter the whole . . .": William S. White, "House Group Votes a New Bill to Curb Powers of Unions," *New York Times*, April 12, 1947, 1.

p. 92, "Such a step . . .": Louis Stark, "Curbs on Labor Hit by Schwellenbach," *New York Times*, January 29, 1947, 1.

p. 92, "The Association . . .": Louis Stark, "Curbs on Labor Hit by Schwellenbach."

pp. 93–94, "The union leader…": Louis Stark, "Hits Government: The Mine Workers Chief Testifying Before Senate Labor Committee," *New York Times*, March 8, 1947, 1.

p. 94, "In other testimony . . .": Louis Stark, "Save Bargaining, Keep Peace in Industry, Says NLRB Head," *New York Times*, March 7, 1947, 1.

p. 95, "resent and reject . . .": A. H. Raskin, "CIO Pushes Action for Curb on Reds," *New York Times*, December 1, 1946, 1.

p. 95, "no threat of reprisal . . .": Louis Stark, "Senators to Split over Labor Curbs," *New York Times*, April 6, 1947, 7.

p. 96, "one of the most . . .": Joseph A. Loftus, "Full Overhauling of Wagner Act Is Approved by Senate Committee," *New York Times*, April 18, 1947, 1.

p. 98, "In April the union's . . .": "Labor Clouds," *New York Times*, April 6, 1947, E1.

p. 98, "On April 22 . . .": "AFL to Fight Curbs by Publicity Drive," *New York Times*, April 23, 1947, 17.

pp. 98–99, "Taft argued . . .": William S. White, "Ives Leads Revolt," *New York Times*, May 8, 1947, 1.

p. 99, "This amendment . . .": White, "Ives Leads Revolt."

p. 99, "He told his colleagues . . .": William S. White, "Bill Passed, 68–24," *New York Times*, May 14, 1947, 1.

p. 101, "fair to workers . . .": William S. White, "Bipartisan Sweep," *New York Times*, June 6, 1947, 1.

p. 102, "Senator Murray mourned . . .": William S. White, "Opposition Is Weak," *New York Times*, June 7, 1947, 1.

p. 102, "No one could . . .": Editorial, "An 'Extreme' Measure?" *New York Times*, June 10, 1947, C26.

p. 104, "CIO president . . .": A. H. Raskin, "Murray and O'Dwyer Assail Taft-Hartley Measure—Wallace Sends Message—Overflow Crowd Hears Speeches," *New York Times*, June 12, 1947, 1.

p. 104, "He portrayed . . .": Harry S. Truman, "On the Veto of the Taft-Hartley Bill," radio address, June 20, 1947. Miller Center of Public Affairs, University of Virginia. http://millercenter.org/scripps/archive/speeches/detail/3344

p. 105, "Truman said . . .": Harry S. Truman, "On the Veto of the Taft-Hartley Bill,"

p. 105, "Truman sent a final . . .": William S. White, "Truman Plea Fails," *New York Times*, June 24, 1947, 1.

pp. 105–106, "During three hours . . .": William S. White, "Truman Plea Fails."

Chapter Six

p. 108, "The Taft-Hartley Act shut down": Louis Stark, "What the Labor Bill Would Mean to the Unions," *New York Times*, May 25, 1947, E3.

p. 109, "AFL president William Green . . .": Charles Grutzner, "Miners Walk Out," *New York Times*, June 24, 1947, 1.

p. 109, "the first ugly, . . .": National Affairs: "I Wandered Lonely . . .," *Time*, October 27, 1947. www.time.com/time/magazine/article/0,9171,854791,00.html

p. 109, "Unions garnered support . . .": Dulles, *Labor in America*, 360.

pp. 109–110, "In August 1947 . . .": Edward H. Collins, "Economics and Finance," *New York Times*, August 18, 1947, 25.

p. 110, "turn out our . . .": W. H. Lawrence, "Taft Act Reprisal Wide Vote Factor,"

New York Times, November 30, 1948, 24.

p. 113, "Both proponents . . .": Louis Stark, "Coal Dispute Brings Demand for New Law," *New York Times*, March 4, 1950, 145.

p. 114, "The statute does . . .": *Steelworkers* v. *United States*, 361 U.S. 39 (1959).

p. 114, "Steel officials . . .": "The Economy: Aspirin for Steel," *Time*, November 16, 1959. www.time.com/time/magazine/article/0,9171,811417-1,00.html

p. 116, "In his message . . .": Gerald Ford, "Veto of a Common Situs Picketing Bill," January 2, 1976. John T. Woolley and Gerhard Peters, *The American Presidency Project* [online]. Santa Barbara, CA. www.presidency.ucsb.edu/ws/?pid=5910

p. 117, "Clinton declared . . .": William J. Clinton, "Message to the House of Representatives Returning Without Approval the Teamwork for Employees and Managers Act of 1995," July 30, 1996. John T. Woolley and Gerhard Peters, *The American Presidency Project* [online]. Santa Barbara, CA. www.presidency.ucsb.edu/ws/?pid=53139

p. 117, "In 2009 fewer . . .": Lydia Saad, "Labor Unions See Sharp Slide in U.S. Public Support," Gallup, September 3, 2009. www.gallup.com/poll/122744/Labor-Unions-Sharp-Slide-Public-Support.aspx

pp. 117–118, "In 2009 only . . .": Steven Greenhouse, "Union Membership Up Sharply in 2008, Report Says," *New York Times* , January 28, 2009, A18.

p. 119, "The Bureau of Labor . . .:" Bureau of Labor Statistics, "Table 1. Work stoppages involving 1,000 or more workers, 1947–2009," United States Department of Labor. www.bls.gov/news.release/wkstp.t01.htm

p. 119, "Presidents have used . . .": "Mine Back-to-Work Order Expires After Judge Refuses to Extend It," *New York Times*, March 18, 1978, 12.

p. 122, "Elizabeth Shuler, . . .": Steven Greenhouse, "Survey Finds Deep Shift in the Make-Up of Unions," *New York Times*, November 10, 2009, B5.

pp. 122–123, "Bureau of Labor records . . .": Steven Greenhouse, "Union Membership Up Sharply in 2008, Report Says," *New York Times*, January 28, 2009, A18.

p. 123, "We've seen . . .": Steven Greenhouse, "Survey Finds Deep Shift in the Make-Up of Unions," *New York Times*, November 10, 2009, B5.

p. 123, "The fastest growth . . .": Linda Lowen, "Women Union Members—The Changing Face of Union Membership," About.com. http://womensissues.about.com/od/womeninthework force/a/WomenUnionMemb.htm

p. 123, "Unions have been . . .": Steven Greenhouse, "Survey Finds Deep Shift in the Make-Up of Unions," *New York Times*, November 10, 2009, B5.

p. 123, "During the presidential . . .": Kim Moody, "Are U.S. Unions Ready for the Challenge of a New Period?" *New Politics*, 12:3, Summer 2009. http://newpolitics.mayfirst.org/fromthearchives?nid=89

p. 123, "If organized labor . . .": Kim Moody, "Are U.S. Unions Ready for the Challenge of a New Period?"

All websites were accurate and accessible as of November 19, 2010.

Further Information

AUDIO/VIDEO

The Legislative Branch. Wynnewood, PA: Schlessinger Media, 2002 (video).

A Nation in Turmoil. Wynnewood, PA: Schlessinger Media, 1996 (video).

U.S. Labor and Industrial History World Wide Web Audio Archive, Department of History, University at Albany, State University of New York. www.albany.edu/history/LaborAudio (various audio recordings)

BOOKS

Bridegam, Martha. *Unions and Labor Laws.* Broomall, PA: Chelsea House Publishers, 2009.

Hile, Kevin. *Cesar Chavez: UFW Labor Leader.* San Diego: Lucent Books, 2008.

Keller, Emily. *Frances Perkins: First Woman Cabinet Member.* Greensboro, NC: Morgan Reynolds Publishing, 2006.

Lindop, Edmund, and Margaret J. Goldstein. *America in the 1940s.* Brookfield, CT: Twenty-First Century Books, 2009.

Marsico, Katie. *The Triangle Shirtwaist Factory Fire: Its Legacy of Labor Rights.* New York: Benchmark Books, 2009.

McNeese, Tim. *The Labor Movement: Unionizing America.* Broomall, PA: Chelsea House Publishers, 2007.

Miller, Debra A. *Dolores Huerta, Labor Leader.* San Diego: Lucent Books, 2006.

Scheppler, Bill. *How a Law Is Passed.* Broomall, PA: Chelsea House Publishers, 2007.

Skurzynski, Gloria. *Sweat and Blood: A History of U.S. Labor Unions.* Brookfield, CT: Twenty-First Century Books, 2008.

Wager, Viqi, ed. *Labor Unions.* Farmington Hills, MI: Greenhaven Press, 2007.

Taft-Hartley Act

WEBSITES

America.gov, U.S. Department of State
www.america.gov/amlife/government.html

American Federation of Labor–Congress of Industrial Organizations
www.aflcio.org

American Presidents, Miller Center of Public Affairs
http://millercenter.org/academic/americanpresident

Department of Labor website
www.dol.gov

Dirksen Congressional Center
www.congresslink.org

Library of Congress
www.loc.gov/index.html

Library of Congress, American Memory
http://memory.loc.gov/ammem/index.html

National Archives
www.archives.gov

National Institute for Labor Relations Research
www.nilrr.org

National Labor Relations Board
www.nlrb.gov

Our Documents Initiative
www.ourdocuments.gov/index.php?flash=true&

Taft-Hartley Act
www.historycentral.com/documents/Tafthatley.html

Harry S. Truman Library and Museum
www.trumanlibrary.org

U.S. House of Representatives
www.house.gov

U.S. Senate
www.senate.gov

All websites were accurate and accessible as of November 19, 2010.

Bibliography

ARTICLES

"Aspirin for Steel," *Time*, November 16, 1959. www.time.com/time/magazine/article/0,9171,811417-1,00.html

Baird, Charles W. "Policy Analysis: The Permissible Uses of Forced Union Dues: From Hanson to Beck." Cato Institute, 1992. www.cato.org/pubs/pas/pa-174.html

"Battle of the Overpass, May 26, 1937." Ford Motor Company Chronology, Henry Ford Museum. www.thehenryford.org/exhibits/fmc/battle.asp

Berman, Edward. "The Supreme Court Interprets the Railway Labor Act," *The American Economic Review*, 20, December 1930, 619–639.

Bernstein, Irving. "Americans in Depression and War." History at the Department of Labor. www.dol.gov/oasam/programs/history/chapter5.htm

Bork, William. "Massacre at Republic Steel." Illinois Labor History Society. www.kentlaw.edu/ilhs/republic.htm

Brown, James D. Jr. "A Curriculum of United States Labor History for Teacher," Illinois Labor History Society. www.kentlaw.edu/ilhs/curricul.htm

Bruno, Robert. "Presidential Labor Regimes: Democrats from Roosevelt to Clinton." IRRA's Proceedings of the Fiftieth Annual Meeting, Industrial Relations Research Association, January 3–5, 1998.

Bureau of Labor Statistics. "Table 1. Work stoppages involving 1,000 or more workers, 1947–2009." United States Department of Labor. www.bls.gov/news.release/wkstp.t01.htm

"Congress: Squaring Off Over 14(b)," *Time*, October 1, 1965. www.time.com/time/magazine/article/0,9171,834404-1,00.html

"Definitions for Common Labor Terms," International Brotherhood of Teamsters. www.teamster.org/content/definitions-common-labor-terms

"Dockworkers Moving Cargo Through Snarled Ports After Taft-Hartley Injunction," AFL-CIO online, October 21, 2002. http://staging.aflcio.org/aboutus/ns10212002.cfm

"8-Hour Work Day," American Memory, Library of Congress. http://memory.loc.gov/ammem/today/aug20.html

"Frances Perkins: Politics and Public Service, 1882-1965," *Online Highways.* www.u-s-history.com/pages/h1603.html

"A History of Unemployment Insurance Legislation in the United States and New York State, 1935–1998." New York (State) Department of Labor, October 1999. www.nysl.nysed.gov/scandoclinks/ocm42538932.htm

"History 101, Right to Work: A Winning Issue." National Institute for Labor Relations Research, 2002. www.nilrr.org/node/62

"I Wandered Lonely...," *Time*, October 27, 1947. www.time.com/time/magazine/article/0,9171,854791,00.html

"Knights of Labor," *NWtravel Magazine Online.* www.u-s-history.com/pages/h933.html

LeRoy, Michael H. and John H. Johnson IV, "Death by Lethal Injunction: National Emergency Strikes Under the Taft-Hartley Act and the Moribund Right to Strike," *Arizona Law Review*, 43:1, 2001.

Ludwig, Jordan. "The Passage and Events Surrounding the Taft-Hartley Act: An Analysis," *Janus*, Spring 2007, 1–2. www.janus.umd.edu

"Major Work Stoppages in 2005," Bureau of Labor Statistics, United States Department of Labor, March 2, 2006. www.bls.gov/news.release/archives/wkstp_03022006.pdf

"Majority Favor a New Labor Union Law." Gallup. www.gallup.com/video/116860/Majority-Favor-New-Labor-Union-Law.aspx

McGovern, George S. "The 'Free Choice' Act Is Anything But," *Wall Street Journal*, May 7, 2009, A15.

———. "My Party Should Respect Secret Union Ballots," *Wall Street Journal*, August 8, 2008, A13.

Merriam-Webster's Online Dictionary. www.merriam-webster.com/

"Mother Jones," Deb-Jones-Douglass Institute website. www.djdinstitute.org/jones.html

"National Affairs: Taft-Hartley: How It Works & Has Worked," *Time*, October 19, 1959. www.time.com/time/magazine/article/0,9171,869269,00.html

New York Times, selected articles (see Notes).

Newman, Pauline. "Letters to Michel and Hugh from P.M. Newman," May 1951.

Kheel Center for Labor-Management Documentation and Archives, Cornell University ILR School. www.ilr.cornell.edu/trianglefire/texts/letters/newman_letter.html?location=Sweatshops+and+Strikes

"People & Events: Industrial Workers of the World," American Experience, Public Broadcasting Service. www.pbs.org/wgbh/americanexperience/

"Preamble and Declaration of Principles of the Knights of Labor of America," *Journal of United Labor*, 1885, American Memory, Library of Congress. http://memory.loc.gov/ammem/index.html

Saad, Lydia "Labor Unions See Sharp Slide in U.S. Public Support." Gallup, September 3, 2009. www.gallup.com/poll/122744/Labor-Unions-Sharp-Slide-Public-Support.aspx

Stolberg, Benjamin. "Big Steel, Little Steel, and C. I. O. ," *The Nation*, July 31, 1937, 145, 119–123.

"Taft-Hartley: How It Works and Has Worked," *Time*, October 19, 1959. www.time.com/time/magazine/article/0,9171,869269,00.html

Wagner, Steven. "How Did the Taft-Hartley Act Come About?" George Mason University's History News Network, October 14, 2002. http://hnn.us/articles/1036.html

"The Uprising of 20,000 and the Triangle Shirtwaist Fire." AFL–CIO. www.afl-cio.org/aboutus/history/history/uprising_fire.cfm

Woolley, John T. and Gerhard Peters. "The American Presidency Project" [online]. Santa Barbara, CA. www.presidency.ucsb.edu

Zahavi, Gerald. "A History of Working People in Tory and Cohoes, New York: A Time Line, 1600s to 1977," University at Albany History Department. www.albany.edu/history/riverspark.html

BOOKS/BOOKLETS

Altgeld, John. *Live Questions*. Chicago: George S. Bowen and Son, 1899.

Atkinson, Linda. *Mother Jones: The Most Dangerous Woman in America*. New York: Crown Publishers Inc., 1978.

Clark, Gordon L. *Unions and Communities Under Siege: American Communities and the Crisis of Organized Labor*. New York: Cambridge University Press, 1989.

Cox, Archibald, et al., *Cases and Materials on Labor Law*, 11th ed. Eagan, MN: Foundation Press, 1991.

Dulles, Foster Rhea. *Labor in America: A History*. New York: Thomas Y. Crowell Company, 1966. Rev. by Melvyn Dubofsky. Wheeling, Illinois: Harlan Davidson, 2004.

Green, James R. *Death in the Haymarket: A Story of Chicago, the First Labor Movement, and the Bombing that Divided Gilded Age America.* New York: Pantheon, 2006.

Johnson, Charles W. *How Our Laws Are Made.* Washington, DC: Governmental Printing Office, 1998.

Lambert, Josiah Bartlett. *"If the Workers Took a Notion": The Right to Strike and American Political Development.* Ithaca, NY: ILR Press/Cornell University Press, 2005.

Lee, R. Alton. *Truman and Taft-Hartley: A Question of Mandate.* Lexington, KY: University of Kentucky Press, 1966.

Millis, Harry A., and Emily Clark Brown. *From the Wagner Act to Taft-Hartley: A Study of National Labor Policy and Labor Relations.* Chicago: University of Chicago Press, 1950.

Orleck, Annelise. *Common Sense and a Little Fire: Women and Working-Class Politics in the United States, 1900–1965.* Chapel Hill, NC: University of North Carolina Press, 1995.

Taylor, George W. *Government Regulations of Industrial Relations.* New York: Prentiss-Hall Inc., 1948.

Vorse, Mary Heaton. *Labor's New Millions.* New York: Modern Age Books Inc., 1938. Internet Archive, www.archive.org/stream/laborsnewmillion00vorsrich/laborsnewmillion00vorsrich_djvu.txt

COURT CASES

Adair v. *United States*, 208 U.S. 161 (1898).

American Communications Association v. *Douds*, 339 U.S. 382 (1950).

Commonwealth v. *Hunt*, 45 Mass. 111 (1842)

Coronado Coal Company v. *United Mine Workers*, 268 U.S. 295 (1925).

Hunt v. *Crumboch*, 325 US 821 (1945).

Lochner v. *New York*, 198 U.S. 45 (1905).

Loewe v. *Lawlor*, 208 U.S. 274 (1908).

National Labor Relations Board v. *Jones and Laughlin Steel Corporation*, 301 U.S. 1 (1937).

NLRB v. *Mackay Radio*, 304 US 345–46 (1938).

Schechter Poultry Corporation v. *United States*, 295 U.S. 495 (1935).

Steelworkers v. *United States*, 361 U.S. 39 (1959).

Texas & New Orleans Railroad Company v. *Brotherhood of Railway & Steamship Clerks*, 281 US 548 (1930).

Truax v. *Corrigan*, 257 US 312 (1921).

United Mine Workers v. *Coronado Coal Company*, 259 U.S. 344 (1922).

United Mine Workers et al v. *Red Jacket Consolidated Coal & Coke Co.*, 18 F. 2d 839 (C.C.A. 4, 1927).

United States v. *Brown*, 381 U.S. 437 (1965).

United States v. *United Mine Workers*, 330 U.S. 258 (1947).

West Coast Hotel Company v. *Parrish*, 300 U.S. 379 (1937).

DOCUMENTS/SPEECHES
Truman, Harry S. "On the Veto of the Taft-Hartley Bill," radio address, June 20, 1947. Miller Center of Public Affairs, University of Virginia. http://millercenter.org/scripps/archive/speeches/detail/3344

————. "Special Message to the Congress on the Steel Strike," John T. Woolley and Gerhard Peters, *The American Presidency Project* [online]. Santa Barbara, CA, June 10, 1952. www.presidency.ucsb.edu/ws/?pid=14152

————. "State of the Union Address," January 6, 1947. http://teachingamericanhistory.org/library/index.asp?document=1360

U.S. LAWS
Clayton Antitrust Act of 1914
www.historycentral.com/documents/Clayton.html

National Industrial Recovery Act, 1933
[Electronic Records]; National Archives at College Park, College Park, MD. www.ourdocuments.gov/doc.php?doc=66

National Labor Relations Act (Wagner Act), 1935
[Electronic Records]; National Archives at College Park, College Park, MD. www.ourdocuments.gov/doc.php?flash=old&doc=67

Labor Management Relations Act of 1947 (Taft-Hartley Act)
www.law.cornell.edu/uscode/29/usc_sup_01_29_10_7.html
http://vi.uh.edu/pages/buzzmat/tafthartley.html

Labor-Management Reporting and Disclosure Act of 1959 (Landrum-Griffin Act), 29 USCA §401 et seq.
www.law.cornell.edu/uscode/29/usc_sup_01_29_10_7_20_II.html

Norris-La Guardia Anti-Injunction Act, 47 U.S. Stat. 70.

Sherman Antitrust Act, 15 U.S.C. (1890).

[Electronic Records]; National Archives at College Park, College Park, MD. www. ourdocuments.gov/doc.php?flash=old&doc=51

WEBSITES

U.S. Department of State
http://uspolitics.america.gov/uspolitics/government/index.html

American Federation of Labor–Congress of Industrial Organizations
www.aflcio.org

American President: Harry S. Truman, Miller Center of Public Affairs
http://millercenter.org/academic/americanpresident/truman

Department of Labor
www.dol.gov

Dirksen Congressional Center
www.congresslink.org/

History Matters American Social History Project
http://historymatters.gmu.edu

Library of Congress, American Memory
http://memory.loc.gov/ammem/index.html

Library of Congress, Primary Documents in American History
www.loc.gov/rr/program/bib/ourdocs/

National Archives
www.archives.gov

National Institute for Labor Relations Research
www.nilrr.org

National Labor Relations Board
www.nlrb.gov

Our Documents Initiative
www.ourdocuments.gov

Taft-Hartley Law
www.historycentral.com/documents/Tafthatley.html

Harry S. Truman Library and Museum
www.trumanlibrary.org/

U.S. Congress
www.house.gov (House)
www.senate.gov (Senate)

All websites were accurate and accessible as of November 19, 2010.

Index

Page numbers in **boldface** are illustrations.

About the Author

SUSAN DUDLEY GOLD has worked as a reporter for a daily newspaper, managing editor of two statewide business magazines, and freelance writer for several regional publications. She has written more than four dozen books for middle-school and high-school students on a variety of topics, including American history, health issues, law, and space.

Gold has won numerous awards for her work, including most recently the selection of *Loving* v. *Virginia: Lifting the Ban Against Interracial Marriage*, part of Marshall Cavendish's Supreme Court Milestones series, as one of the Notable Social Studies Trade Books for Young People in 2009. Three other books in that series have received recognition: *United States* v. *Amistad: Slave Ship Mutiny*, selected as a Carter G. Woodson Honor Book in 2008; and *Tinker* v. *Des Moines: Free Speech for Students* in 2008 and *Roberts* v. *Jaycees: Women's Rights* in 2010, both awarded first place in the National Federation of Press Women's communications contest, nonfiction juvenile book category.

Gold has written several titles in the Landmark Legislation series for Marshall Cavendish. She is the author of a number of books on Maine history. She and her husband, John Gold, own and operate a web design and publishing business in Maine. They have one son, Samuel; a granddaughter, Callie; and a grandson, Alexander.